Together After All
Alexis Vance

To Samuel and Matthew,
for showing me what true love is.
May you never stray from your faith.

Contents

Introduction

Together After All is the first installment in the *Tangled in Grace* series.

This book is a Christian based, fictional romance and contains real life situations. Some scenes in this book may be considered upsetting or triggering to some readers.

Some of the trigger warnings include; mentions of alcohol abuse and domestic situations.

Thank you so much for joining me on this journey. I hope you enjoy Coraline's story!

1
Coraline

SCOTTSDALE IS QUIET AND calm at this time in the morning. It's early June and school is out so there's not any traffic right now. It's just me and the road.

I have my windows rolled down and my music turned up. I woke up early enough to do a full face of makeup and eat breakfast before my kids got out of bed. That's pretty much unheard of for us. Today is going to be a great first day, I just know it.

My phone starts ringing and my positive thoughts are interrupted. My heart drops as I recognize the assigned ringtone. I declined the call immediately.

"I do not have time for you to ruin my day Nash," I say quietly to myself as I roll my eyes. I refuse to let him destroy anything else for me or the kids. Including my day today.

I have the normal first day jitters as I make my last turn and pull into the parking lot of the Scottsdale Clinic.

This clinic has been in Scottsdale since the creation of the town. This is the place that I came to my whole life for check ups and sick visits. It's kind of cool that I get to work here now as an adult.

The building itself is a large, two story, brick building with a wrap-around porch. There are rocking chairs lined up by the entrance and various plants and flowers decorate the porch.

Despite the simplicity and nostalgia of the clinic, there is a dire need for good medical care here in this area. Anyone who needs medical treatment comes here first because the nearest hospital is an hour away. A lot of rural citizens don't go to the doctor or hospital when they need to because they either don't want to drive that far or can't afford to.

My phone interrupts my thoughts again but this time it's a text from Shae.

Hey girl! I'm so sorry but I'm running a few minutes late this morning. I just wanted to give you a heads up. I know it's your first day and you'll probably be waiting on me. Love you! <3

Shae is the receptionist at the clinic and also my childhood best friend. We grew up together attending a local church in town, Grace Haven. We've known each other since we were in diapers and we always made sure to keep in touch—even when I moved away.

I hesitantly decide to go back and listen to the voicemail Nash left me since I have some extra time now.

The voicemail starts out with static and a brief moment of silence before Nash's rough voice crackles through my car speakers. I scrunch up my face and cringe.

"Hey...it's me again. Your loving fiancé. Are you ever going to bring my son to see me? I will be expecting–" I roll my eyes again, hang up and turn the car off. That's enough of that.

Narcissists always make everything about themselves. They act like they're the victim and bring everyone else around them down. It's one of the many reasons I decided to leave him—and that was before he went to jail.

When I first met Nash, he seemed to be so perfect. Key word being "seemed".

I was a young, single mom who was working full time at the hospital. I had only ever had one boyfriend before him and that was Harrison's dad, Jesse. I was so deprived of affection that I clung to the first person who showed me any.

Sometimes I wonder how different my life would be if I would've stayed in town—if Jesse would have heard me out and chose us. But, I believe that everything happens for a reason. Even if we don't understand why. I'm sure Jesse has moved on and is chasing his dreams just like I did.

I've tried my best to let go, forgive and move on from my anger. But that's easier said than done. He made his choice. I can't keep holding on to the past.

 I step out of my car, grab my purse, and take a deep breath in. I look over my shoulder and see Shae getting out of her car. She has her short, black hair pulled up with a claw clip and is rocking a pair of pink scrubs.

She wasn't late at all, she was actually right on time.

I picked out my lucky set of jogger scrubs to wear today with my white coat jacket. I can dress pretty much however I'd like to, but I always prefer scrubs. They feel like you're wearing pajamas but they still make you look professional. The fabric is soft, functional and stylish. Plus, I have plenty of pockets—it's a win win.

"Cora! I'm so excited that we finally get to work together and see each other everyday again!"

"Honestly, I am too," I say with a smile. "I'm glad to be back. I'm ready for a fresh start."

"Speaking of fresh starts, look at what I got for you! Your favorite coffee." She leans into her car and pulls out a large iced coffee from the local coffee shop.

"Shae you are an angel sent from God himself!"

"I know," she says as she smirks and gives me a hug. I take the iced coffee and follow Shae up the front porch steps and through the clinic door.

When I first walk into the clinic, I realize that it really hasn't changed that much at all. It still smells the same—slightly of antiseptic with a mix of aged furniture and carpet.

There are leather chairs lined up in the waiting room that are waiting for patients to come and fill them. They still have magazines in the waiting room for patients to occupy themselves with since cell phone service in this town sucks.

As a nurse practitioner I will be helping Dr. Dawson, the owner, by taking over the care of some of his patients. He will still ultimately be over the clinic but now he will have an extra set of hands.

As if on cue, Dr. Dawson walks into the clinic. He has a golden tan, dark hair, and the most flawless skin I've ever seen on a man. He's wearing light blue scrubs with a red fleece jacket. Even though it's summer, he always has a jacket on or with him at all times.

He walks through the lobby and up to the front desk while holding his man purse. It's a running joke with everyone in town because he always keeps a bag full of his favorite drinks with him at all times.

"Good morning ladies. I'm glad to see that you made it Coraline. Let's get this day started, shall we?"

2
Coraline

AFTER A LONG TEN hours of working at the clinic, it's finally time to come home. Since we had to move back to my hometown so abruptly, we're staying in a rental house near Camp Willowbrooke until we find something more permanent.

I walk onto the porch and open the cabin style door.

As soon as I step into the living room, the smoke detector is alarming and I smell something burning.

Harrison and Michael are both running around the entire house like wild animals. There are toy cars and dinosaurs strung everywhere—it looks like a bomb went off.

We moved into the rental house about a week ago and everything is almost unpacked, but there are still quite a few boxes stacked around the house. When you add toys into the mix, it's even worse.

"Hey boys! Hey Gemma! What's on fire?" I shout over the noise of the smoke detector.

"MOMMY!" the boys yell in unison.

I crouch down and they both come running into my arms. I swear there's absolutely nothing better than this. They have the power to make even the worst days better.

The smoke detector is still blaring through the entire house, so I break apart from their embrace and walk into the kitchen to find my sister.

Gemma is fanning smoke from the oven out the window and away from the alarm with an oven mitt. She looks like she's ready to have a mental breakdown. I cover my mouth to hide my smile.

Gemma is the best esthetician in town and has the option to create her own work schedule. She offered to watch the boys for me while I worked today. She's never been married and she doesn't have any kids, unless you count her fur baby, Goose, so watching mine is always an adventure for her.

Gemma's long blonde hair is braided into two messy french braids. She's wearing biker shorts with an oversized t-shirt that is now decorated in flour. Her makeup is still on and looks just like it did when I left this morning, despite all of the chaos—I need to find out what setting spray she uses.

"We survived." Gemma sighs as she wipes sweat from her brow. "As for the smell and alarm, the boys decided they wanted to help me make some cookies from scratch. Michael was very insistent."

"Something went wrong. I'm not really sure what happened because both of the boys had to go to the bathroom at the same time and we lost track of time and of how long we had been gone. Next thing I know, the smoke detector is blaring and the cookies are smoking in the oven."

I lean in to give her a hug. "I really appreciate you doing this today, even though you did almost burn the house down."

"Anything for you. I know you've got a lot going on in that big head of yours." She lowers her voice and whispers, "I still think you should get them a pet."

I pull away from the hug and look at her with my eyes wide. "The house really would've burnt down if there was an animal here that you had to keep up with too."

My sons have been begging me to let them get a pet. The only reason I haven't yet is because Nash was always so against it.

When we first got together, Nash told me he loved animals and that he would have a whole house full of them if he could. He obviously lied to me because he actually hates them and they don't seem to like him either.

My sister's golden retriever Goose, who wouldn't hurt a fly, would not stop growling at him the first and only time they met each other.

"I have been thinking about it. I can't do it right now though. I have to wait until we move. I'm not sure the owners of the rental property would be okay with us adding another creature of destruction inside of the house."

"You might be surprised," Gemma replies.

The rental house was built with timber logs and even still smells like pine, if you ignore the current burnt cookie smell. The house came fully furnished so all of our furniture from the old house is in storage.

There's a stone fireplace in the living room with a TV mounted on the mantel. The kids have made this area their own hangout fully equipped with their games and favorite movies. There's two cabin style couches with one recliner and it fits us perfectly.

"Do you want to stay and eat dinner, Gemma?"

"Oh no, that's okay. I've got to go home to my fur baby. He misses me. I can practically hear him whining from here." Gemma laughs nervously and then gives each of the boys a hug goodbye.

Once Gemma is gone, I go to my room and change. I pick out my favorite pair of shorts and put my hair up into a messy bun.

I get a wash cloth and wipe off all of my makeup. I do a little bit of post-makeup removal skin care and my stomach growls loudly.

Shoot! I still need to make dinner.

I leave the master bedroom to go check on Harrison and Michael before I start cooking. They're sitting side by side on the living room floor playing a video game on the TV.

Harrison is tall and skinny for his age. His curly, dark hair always looks like a tousled mess no matter what products I use, but he has embraced it.

Michael is my wild child and he's his dads twin. Unlike Harrison, he has straight blond hair and big brown eyes.

"I'm going to get started on dinner. Is there anything you all want to eat?"

"No. Just surprise us," Harrison replies without looking up from the TV.

"Okay, if you say so." I head back into the kitchen. I'm absolutely exhausted.

I open up the fridge and look for inspiration for dinner. I'm honestly too tired to make anything from scratch and I really need to go to the store. This is probably one of my least favorite parts about being an adult—picking out what's for dinner every night.

After standing with the refrigerator door open for entirely too long, I decided that a frozen pizza sounds like a wonderful idea. It's something simple and easy, and both of the boys will eat it. I pull our favorite brand of frozen pizza out of the freezer and put it on the counter for now.

Before I preheat the oven, I pull out the burnt cookies. It's been at least an hour since Gemma left so they're completely cooled down. I throw them straight into the trash.

The burnt cookie smell is almost unbearable now that they're out of the oven. I feel like I can't concentrate if my house smells bad and I know exactly how to fix it.

I go to the cabinet, pull out my favorite candle and then light it. The candle has a fall scent, but it makes any place smell and feel like home—no matter the time of year.

It's called *Spice of Life*. It smells like warm pancakes with maple syrup and hints of cinnamon. It's only sold locally in town and Gemma usually keeps it in stock at her salon.

I hit the preheat button on the stove and decide to clean up the kitchen while I wait. There's not many things that feel better than a clean house and the smell of a candle.

After I finish a sink full of dishes, I realize that I never heard the oven beep. I must've just been in my head too much and unintentionally ignored it.

As I lower the pizza onto the rack, I realize that the oven is still room temperature and never preheated—it's not even warm.

I try to turn it off and back on again. Nothing happens. Great. My temper is already short from being so overstimulated today and this makes me want to explode.

I take a deep breath, shut my eyes and count to ten as I exhale. This is something I've found myself doing more of since becoming a single parent. I can do this. I will do this.

I pull the oven out from the wall and unplug it. I wait a few minutes and then I plug it back in. Nothing happens, again.

I let out another heavy breath.

I'm going to have to get in-touch with the owners, Henry and Mira Jacobs. They own most of the rental houses in Scottsdale and are also old family friends of my grandparents.

I shoot Henry a text and let him know what happened. Maybe he can swing by this evening and fix it.

A reply bounces back almost immediately.

I am so sorry Coraline. Mira and I are out of town for the week on vacation. I will send someone over. He will take care of it.

He? Oh well, I don't really care who fixes it as long as I can make something for dinner tonight.

Thank you, Henry!   I appreciate it!

I walk back into the living room and notice that the boys are still playing their favorite racing game. I just started a new fantasy romance series the other day but I haven't had much time to enjoy it with everything that's going on. I silently pull my book out and make myself comfortable. If I'm too loud and Michael see's the book, it's game over for my plans of reading anything.

I finish reading two pages when a knock at the door interrupts my thoughts—I will never get to read this book. I slam my book shut and get up from the couch to answer the door.

As I'm walking, whoever is at the front door starts a series of harder knocks. If I wasn't annoyed before, I definitely am now.

Who in the world is it and why are they so impatient?

I open the door and my stomach drops. The guy that Henry sent over to fix my stove is none other than Jesse Cooper. I haven't seen or heard from him since I broke up with him seven years ago.

My face suddenly feels too hot and my ears start to ring as my adrenaline skyrockets—I think I might pass out.

Jesse is standing in the door frame of my house mirroring my look of surprise. He looks just like I remember him, but somehow more.

He stands at around six foot four or five, which is something I always loved about him. His curly hair is still dark and messy and his eyes are the same icy shade of blue.

His skin is sun-kissed and he looks a little rugged but unfortunately for me, still extremely good looking. I mean seriously, how is he still so attractive? It's not fair.

My brain has gone completely blank and I feel like I've forgotten how to speak.

"Mom! Who's at the door?" Harrison shouts. "Is Gemma back?"

Reality comes crashing back into me at full speed. I put my hands behind my back, unsure of what to do with them and suddenly feeling self conscious. I thought this day couldn't get any worse but apparently I was wrong.

"Cora? Forgive me, I wasn't expecting to see you. I didn't even know you were back in town," Jesse pauses and clears his throat. "Henry called me about an oven that wasn't working and I told him I would come check it out."

"Oh right! The oven." I laugh nervously. "Please come in."

It turns out that my voice does in fact still work. I step aside and let Jesse inside of the house.

It was at that moment that I remembered the house is still scattered with toys and I look like a bridge troll. He probably thinks I'm a total slob. Great.

3
Jesse

MY HEART IS BEATING so loud in my body. It's a miracle that I can hear anything at all.

Coraline Jennings, the girl who absolutely broke my heart and shattered the remaining pieces, is standing in front of me. I don't have time to process this feeling yet. I have to put my feelings to the side, do my job like the professional I am, and then I can leave—seems simple enough.

As I step inside of the house, I notice two little boys in the living room playing games and giggling. My stomach plummets and I feel kind of sick.

I look around the room to see if there's a husband or boyfriend anywhere. I don't see anyone else. I also notice that she's not wearing a ring on a very important finger.

Cora is still as stunning as I remember her to be. Five foot seven, with honey colored eyes and full lips. Her beauty has always seemed so effortless. Why am I thinking about her beauty? It's been years, I thought I was over her.

"Are these boys yours?" I ask and immediately wish I hadn't opened my mouth. I know that it's none of my business but I can't help myself.

"Yes. This is Harrison and Michael. They're my sons."

The kids both turn around at the same time and it suddenly feels hard to breathe again. Is it just me, or does the older boy look familiar? He has the same kind of hair as me, but his eyes look just like Cora's. Nope. There's no way. That's not possible.

I lock eyes with the older boy and give him a small smile. He glares at me in return. I turn my attention toward the younger boy and he gives me a big smile and waves. You can tell they're brothers but they really don't look too much alike.

"Hi guys, my name is Jesse. I'm here to fix the oven."

"Do you know my mom?" The younger boy asks innocently.

"Sort of. We went to school together a long time ago."

Coraline turns towards me, sensing my discomfort. "Okay boys back to your games. Man, I am starving! Why don't we get you to the kitchen Jesse?"

"That sounds like a great idea." I follow her out of the living room.

"Don't mind the mess. I started a new job today and Gemma was here with the boys."

Honestly I'm too overwhelmed to notice much of anything at the moment. When I allow myself to look around, I do see that there are toys scattered everywhere.

"Eh, it doesn't bother me." I shrug my shoulders. "So, a new job? Are you back in town for good? Not just visiting?"

"Uh, yeah. I guess so," she replies while avoiding eye contact. "I know this rental is temporary, but we're staying here until I find something more permanent."

"I see. Well, welcome back." I cross my arms over my chest.

"It's good to be back." She finally looks towards me. "This town is perfect for my family right now and this house is so close to the campground. It was a no-brainer on if I wanted to rent it or not."

"My favorite thing about the house, besides the location, is the view from the kitchen." She longingly glances out the window and I follow her gaze. "It has the best view of the lake. If I didn't have to go to work, it would feel like we're on vacation."

What she probably doesn't realize is that my lakeside house is highly visible from that very window. I helped design the cabin and it was one of my favorite finishing touches.

It's a miracle that my legs haven't given out at this point. They feel like jello. I wonder if she notices that I'm an absolute ball of nerves.

"I see you still have excellent taste in candles," I comment, trying to break the ice again.

"Some things never change," she says with a playful shrug.

I nod my head in agreement. "Soo... Henry explained what happened on the phone. I will get my tools in here and see what I can do, then I'll be out of your hair."

"Cool," she says as she turns around to go back to the living room.

Once she's gone, I let out a breath that I didn't realize I had been holding.

My hands are shaking by the time I bend down to take a look at the oven. What is the matter with me? She's just a girl that I used to know. She should not be affecting me this much. I've got to get it together.

I grab my tool bag and mess around with the oven to see what's wrong with it. I notice that the oven has already been pulled out from the wall. Typical Cora, always so headstrong and determined—I guess some things don't change after-all.

I do this repairman job as a side gig and to help out Henry Jacobs. I can afford not to work, thanks to software that I created and sold out to a big company a few years ago, but I like to help others out whenever I can.

That's the beautiful thing about Scottsdale, we're all one big family. When someone needs something, we all pitch in to help. If we can't help, then we know exactly who to call.

After about twenty minutes, I finally get the oven back up and running. I gather up all of my tools, clean up my mess and start making my way to the living room.

When I round the corner, I notice that Cora is on the floor playing with her kids. I unintentionally slow my steps so I can watch them. They're playing with cars and dinosaurs and having some sort of battle.

"Mom, when is my dad coming home?" the youngest boy asks softly as he moves his car back and forth.

"Baby, your dad did some bad things, and he has to go away for a while. You might still get to visit him but it won't ever be like it used to be."

I take that as my sign to make my presence known before the conversation goes any further. I clear my throat loudly. "I got the oven working again. I'll let Henry know— hopefully, you won't have any more issues."

"Thank you," she says as she gives me a tight smile.

"I know you were planning on cooking, but why don't I go and pick you all up something to eat?" I suggest. "It wouldn't be any trouble at all."

"We wouldn't want to keep you any later than we already have. I'm sure someone's waiting for you to get home and I don't want to be the reason you're late," she replies. "I appreciate your help, and the offer."

I nod, deciding that's her polite way of telling me to leave. What she doesn't know is that my house is a football field away from hers. And there's no-one waiting on me at home— just Lucy, my German shepherd.

I've had a few girlfriends here and there, but nothing serious. I always found a reason to end things before they went too far. Cora is the only girl who ever made me feel something. After the way she shattered my heart, I pushed girls away on purpose. I never wanted to feel that kind of pain again.

I step out of the house and climb into my truck. For awhile, I just sit in silence, staring at the steering wheel. It doesn't seem fair— her family is inside, weighed down by sadness, while out here the world is bright, happy, and beautiful.

I can't help but wonder what her kids' father did. How did he treat her? How did he treat the kids? Where is he now? She's practically a stranger to me, why do I care so much?

I shake my head and start the truck. I back out of the driveway and head back home.

My house is a lakeside cabin, tucked on about two acres of open land, just off the road to Camp Willowbrooke. The only other house nearby just so happens to be the rental where Cora's staying.

I pull in my driveway and as soon as Lucy sees my truck, her head pops up and her tail starts wagging. She's sitting on the front porch swing, soaking up the sun and waiting for me to get back home.

I rescued Lucy from the local animal shelter when she was just a little pup. That was four years ago now and she's been my best friend ever since. She's the one and only woman in my life.

I exit the truck and walk over to her. As she leans against me, I rub her favorite spot behind her ear and I kiss the top of her head.

I unlock the front door and step inside. Kicking off my boots, I collapse on the couch and turn the tv on.

My favorite things to watch are classic movies from the seventies and eighties. Tonight, I decide on *Back to the Future,* my favorite comfort movie. I've seen it at-least a hundred times, but it never fails to help me unwind.

As the movie starts, I pull out my phone and mindlessly scroll through social media. I try to focus, but I can't shake the thoughts of Cora and her two sons.

Being the good guy I am, I order them some dinner— along with some sweet treats— and have it delivered to their house. Anonymously, of course. Hopefully it'll put a smile on all of their faces.

4
Coraline

I FEEL LIKE THE kids and I are constantly walking on eggshells. I don't understand why Nash gets so upset so easily. I know I need to get us away from him, but I can't yet.

I've been secretly trying to withdraw some cash, a little at a time, hoping Nash won't notice. He watches our bank account like a hawk.

He'll blow his paychecks on gambling and alcohol without a second thought, and yet if I spend less than ten dollars on the kids for a meal from a fastfood place, he jumps down my throat.

It's eleven p.m. on a school night, and the boys and I are in their bed. They look so peaceful when they sleep. Lately, I've been spending more and more nights with them in their room. I just can't stand the smell of liquor on Nash anymore.

I keep praying that he'll change and that things will get better. At this point, I honestly feel like God has forgotten about me as I live in this hell on earth.

Nash used to drink occasionally when we first got together— mainly just on the weekend or socially— but it's gotten so much worse this past year. He's already on his second DUI and I told him I wouldn't bail him out again if he got another one.

"CORALINE!" Nash yells in a slurred voice and I flinch. "Where are you baby?" I hear him stumbling around in the kitchen— throwing things around. He acts like a giant drunken toddler when he's mad.

I say a quiet prayer that he doesn't wake up the kids. I don't care what he does to me, but I don't ever want them to be involved.

I can hear him cussing as he continues to trash the kitchen. I know if I don't go to him now, he will continue to spiral.

I turn on the kids' TV, setting it to a white noise channel, and raise the volume so they won't hear what's about to happen. Quietly, I slip out of their bedroom and tiptoe into the kitchen.

I smell him before I see him. Nash has a bottle of liquor in his hands and is drinking it like it's water. He's so drunk that he can't even stand up straight. He's swaying back and forth and his eyes are glassy and bloodshot.

"Shh shh. I'm right here, Nash. I didn't go anywhere," I attempt to calm him down and wrap him up in an embrace. He starts to sob and drool on my shoulder.

Then, suddenly, he stops crying.

"You weren't in my bed waiting for me."

My breath catches in my throat and tears well in my eyes. I just pray the kids can sleep through his antics tonight. This is the second time this week he's done this.

It honestly scares me how quickly he can switch like that. I never know what he's going to do or say, but I always know it's not going to be good when he gets like this.

I know that the best thing to do right now is to try to distract him and de-escalate the situation. Sometimes it works, most of the time it doesn't.

"Baby look at me," I say as I wipe my eyes and take his hands in mine. "Shh. It's okay. Let's go to bed now. I'll go with you." I press a kiss to his cheek and cringe internally.

He follows me to the bedroom. My stomach clenches in dread. I can't keep doing this. I've got to get out of this prison and away from him.

5
Coraline

JESSE'S BEEN GONE FOR at least forty-five minutes, and I can't stop pacing. When I decided to move back to Scottsdale, I knew there was a chance Jesse and I would cross paths, but I didn't expect it to happen this soon.

I can't believe he acted like he had no idea who Harrison was.

He never replied to or acknowledged my letter all those years ago. I accepted that he didn't want anything to do with Harrison, and I moved on with my life.

Harrison is so loved. He has been since the moment I found out about him. Once the initial shock of being pregnant out of wedlock wore off, Granna and Pappy, my grandparents who raised me, got excited. They've spoiled both of my boys enough to make up for Jesse and his family not being in Harrison's life.

Nash never treated Harrison the same way he treated Michael.

When we first started dating, he was so good about including Harrison in everything we did. But once Michael was born, it was like something changed. I could feel the difference in how he treated them.

Harrison knows that Nash isn't his real dad. He doesn't fully understand the concept, but he understands as much as a six-year-old can.

Harrison's always worried about everyone but himself. He has the biggest, kindest heart in the world. I can't wrap my head around why Jesse wouldn't want to know him. It doesn't make sense to me. Why did he choose to stay out of his life? How could someone do that to a baby that they helped create?

I need to do something to distract myself and take my mind off Jesse. I get up and walk over to the stack of boxes in my room, starting to unpack some more.

The bedroom I'm staying in is decorated with typical cabin-style décor—just like you'd find in a Tennessee vacation cabin. Little black bear prints and figurines are scattered around the room.

The bed has a red and black quilted blanket, with matching plaid pillows. It's cheesy, but it feels cozy, and I secretly love it.

I pick up a box from the top of the stack and sit it on the bed to open it. I peel back all of the packing tape and rip the cardboard apart. When I finally get the box open, the first thing I see is a picture of me and Jesse.

I think this picture was taken during our junior year of high school. The Scottsdale Eagles had just won the biggest game of the year. I was wearing my full cheerleading outfit with a giant bow in my hair and Jesse was in his football gear.

We were hugging, and I was kissing his cheek. We were young and in love. I used to cherish this picture, remembering how happy we were in it. It was one of the best nights of our lives back then.

How ironic is it that I'd find my box of memories when I was trying so hard not to reminisce? I reach for another picture of us when a soft knock sounds at the door.

"Mommy, there's someone outside again."

My heart sinks. I set the picture down on the bed and stand up.

"Okay, I'll go get it, sweetheart. Why don't you and Michael go wash up for dinner? The pizza should be done any minute." I gave him a quick hug before exiting the room.

When I reach the front door, no one's there.

I step out onto the porch and almost trip over a mountain of food.

There's a giant box of cookies, a package of donuts, and three bags of food from local restaurants. They're all addressed to me and my family.

I bend down and inspect the bags. My frown deepens when I notice that there's a receipt attached to one of them.

It has Jesse's name on it.

6
Coraline

Junior Year

"TOUCHDOWN, SCOTTSDALE EAGLES!" THE sports commentator's energetic voice booms throughout the stadium. "What an incredible catch by number twenty-three, Jesse Cooper! I'm telling ya folks, there aren't many young men with as much talent as that one."

Fireworks explode in the endzone, and the football team's players are hyping up the crowd by raising their arms up and down in unison.

The crowd is absolutely electric. They're going wild, ringing cowbells and waving posters of their favorite players.

You can practically feel the excitement in the air—it's tangible.

Tonight is one of the biggest games of the year and it will determine if the Scottsdale Eagles go to the state championship. The football team hasn't gone to state since my parents were in high school, almost twenty years ago.

I'm standing on the sidelines in my cheerleading uniform with my squad as we cheer our hearts out for the boys. There's less than a minute on the clock and it's the fourth quarter. We're only down by a few points and we have a chance to win the game.

Shae is standing beside me. This is one of the few times we don't get separated at a school event. I'm a flyer, and she's my backspot, so we have to be close during our routines, which I love. We're the two kids who cause the entire classroom to get a seating chart because we can't stop talking to each other.

She looks at me and mouths, "It's okay, he's got this." I give her a small, reassuring smile.

Shae knows how nervous I always get for Jesse, especially at games like this. He's been so stressed out about it all week, and I've tried to help him as much as I can.

We turn around to face the crowd and begin one of our cheers. As we go through the motions, my eyes catch Jesse's parents in the stands. His mom, Keri, is staring straight into my soul. I don't know what it is about her, but she's always had this thing against me.

I quickly break her gaze, forcing myself to focus on the rest of the cheer.

I spot my family in the stands cheering along with me and my heart warms. My sister and our grandparents are clapping to the beat of our cheer while the rest of the crowd is focused on the game. They've always been my biggest supporters.

We finish the cheer and turn back around to face the game. There's only ten seconds left on the clock. We have the ball, and this is our last chance.

I start jumping up and down, cheering for Jesse as loudly as I can. I know he can't hear me, but I can't stop myself.

The center snaps the ball to Jesse, and it feels like time slows down. I can hear and feel my own heartbeat in my chest.

"C'mon, Jess, you got this."

He takes a few steps back, prepares to throw the ball to the running back, then pauses.

The clock is down to seven seconds now, and the crowd is roaring.

Suddenly, Jesse takes off, sprinting toward the end zone with everything he's got. The opposing players chase him, but they're falling behind. There's only one second left, and he's so close.

"TOUCHDOWN, SCOTTSDALE EAGLES!" The buzzer sounds, marking the end of the game. He did it! We won!

The team charges the field, and we follow close behind.

Jesse rips off his helmet, and the guys hoist him onto their shoulders, cheering and some even crying happy tears.

I stand to the side, letting him have his moment in the spotlight. He's worked so hard to get here, and he deserves this recognition.

But then, through the sea of players and students, Jesse's eyes lock onto mine. He practically leaps out of their arms and runs straight to me, scooping me up.

"We did it, baby!" He spins us around in a circle.

"I'm so proud of you, Jess!" His lips crash against mine, and in that moment, I don't care who sees us or what anyone thinks. It feels like there's no one else here but him and me. Nothing else matters but the feel of his lips on mine.

"Jesse Cooper! Put that girl down and come hug your mama!" Keri's high-pitched, grating voice cuts through our moment, as it always does. She hardly ever refers to me by my name, even though we've been together for years.

Jesse sets me down and turns to his family. His mom hugs him so tightly that his face is turning red.

"Okay, Keri, that's enough. You're going to break him." Lloyd, Jesse's dad, jokes.

He gives me a side hug and a pat on the back. I've always liked Lloyd—he's always been so kind to me, the complete opposite of Keri.

Shae appears through the crowd and congratulates Jesse on his big win.

"Let me grab a picture of you and Cora, and then you can take one of me and her."

Keri rolls her eyes as Lloyd pulls her away, whispering something in her ear.

Seriously, I don't understand what her problem is. She's Jesse's mom, but she acts like she's in love with him. It's getting weird.

Jesse stands beside me, his arm around me as Shae snaps a few pictures of us posing.

I stand on my tiptoes and plant a kiss on his cheek for the camera.

7
Jesse

I PARK MY TRUCK in the lot of the Scottsdale Diner and step out, heading toward the door to meet Charlie, my best friend.

The diner is sort of a staple in this town. They have the best banana pudding cake in town, but only if it's made by Pamela. She's worked at the diner for as long as I can remember. She's still working at the age of seventy-five! At this point, I think she just genuinely enjoys being here because she refuses to retire.

"Hey man, what's up?" I say as I shake his hand.

"Same old, same old."

Charlie and I have been best friends since middle school. Our dads were best friends too, so it always felt like we were destined to be close. We really grew tight during football season after spending hours on the field together.

He lost his wife a few years ago to cancer. They have a daughter together named Jennifer, or Jenny for short. I think she's the only thing that keeps him going most days.

Jenny is now five years old and is basically my niece. She has me wrapped around her little finger and she knows it.

Charlie and I walk inside of the Scottsdale Diner. As soon as I step in, the warm aroma of home-cooked food hits me, making my stomach growl.

The diner always has a different special running each day, except for Sundays when it's closed for church. The specials rarely ever change, and I know most of them by heart. The country fried steak is my favorite. It practically melts in your mouth. Today is Tuesday, so the special is meatloaf.

The inside of the diner is a little outdated, but that's part of its charm, in my opinion. There are multiple booths with tattered seats that somehow still manage to be comfortable.

In the corner, there's a countertop bar, sitting by itself. The diner doesn't sell alcohol, which some of the younger folks around town don't quite get, but it's just how it's always been. The bar is used as a pickup area for to-go orders instead.

The diner still doesn't have any computer systems, not even a TV. They did recently get a card reader but only because no one carries cash anymore. That's the farthest they've gone with technology. It's refreshing to have to sit and talk to the people you're sitting with and not be distracted by anything.

I follow Charlie to our favorite booth and sit down across from him. I take a deep breath in and look out the window. I can't keep my leg from bouncing—It's an anxiety tic that I've had my whole life.

"What happened?" Charlie asks, his voice low and curious.

"What do you mean?" I force my leg to stay still.

"You know what I mean. What's eating at you?"

"Nothing's eating at me. I'm just fine." I shrug, leaning back in my seat. "Nothing to worry about." My leg starts bouncing again.

"Oh really, nothing at all? Nothing wouldn't happen to be an old flame who moved back into town with her two kids and is working at the clinic?"

I freeze for a second, the words hitting me harder than expected.

"How did you know she was back before I did and why didn't you warn me?"

News travels fast in a small town. He was probably waiting for me to say something to him about it first.

"A little heads up would've been nice, that's all I'm saying." I wipe my sweaty palms on my thighs.

Before Charlie can respond, Pamela comes around the booth to take our order. She still looks fantastic for her age.

She's wearing jeans and a red button-down shirt with her faded waitress apron that is probably older than me, but still well taken care of. Her gray and white streaked hair is pulled into some fancy updo, and her glasses rest on the edge of her nose.

"Why, hello boys! It's so good to see you two back in here today." She has one of those comforting, raspy voices that you can tell she still smokes about a pack a day but is the nicest lady ever.

"Hello, Miss Pamela." Charlie and I reply in unison.

"What can I getcha?" She pulls out her pen and pad, ready to take our order.

"Go ahead and get us the usual." I wink at her.

"I can do that. How's the Camp Willowbrooke party planning going?" She says as she raises an eyebrow.

"It's coming along." I shrug, not wanting to give too much away yet.

"You know, if you need anything, I am more than happy to help."

"I appreciate the offer, but I think right now I'm good. The only thing I need you to do is make sure there's enough of your banana pudding cake to go around."

"I think I can handle that." She playfully slaps my shoulder and walks away.

I've actually been a little stressed out about the celebration. One hundred years is a huge deal and everyone in town will be coming, including Cora's family.

I fold my hands together and sit them on the table. It seems like everything leads back to Cora and her family. I just wish I could get her out of my head. I keep thinking about her two sons and the looks on their faces last night. My heart breaks all over again.

"Do you know anything about Cora's husband?" I ask Charlie quietly.

"Nothing other than they were never actually married, and he's a piece of crap."

"Oh, I just assumed they were. I can't for the life of me understand why anyone would mistreat her or those two innocent boys." I shake my head, my frustration growing. I know that if I was ever given a chance to be in his situation, I would be doing everything possible to keep them happy.

Charlie leans across the table so that only I can hear him. "I heard from the older ladies in town that his name is Nash. I also heard that he initially got a DUI and the same night that he was arrested, Coraline filed domestic assault charges against him. Apparently, that was not his first DUI and he has a major drinking problem."

I don't even know how to respond to that. I instantly see red and I know by the look on Charlie's face that he knows how I feel. How could any man ever think about laying a hand on a woman, especially Cora?

"Did he ever do anything physical to her kids?" I say through gritted teeth, my leg bouncing uncontrollably at this point. I've got to get these feelings under control.

Charlie sits back, stroking his beard as he thinks for a moment. "I haven't heard anything for certain but, I wouldn't put it past him."

The buzzing of the overhead fan and the clinking of silverware only seem to amplify the storm in my mind. My cheeks feel like they're on fire and I'm starting to feel lightheaded.

I force myself to take a deep breath.

Thoughts race through my mind—horrible scenarios of what this man could have done to Cora and the kids. My stomach clenches. I feel like I'm suffocating under the weight of it all.

I can't believe she still has any sort of impact on me, especially after everything. It feels like no matter how much I try to move on, she still holds some piece of me.

8
Coraline

JESSE AND I ARE sitting in our favorite booth at the Scottsdale diner with Charlie and Gemma. My sister tagged along with us after school because our grandparents had some business at the church that they had to take care of.

My grandfather is the pastor at the church we attend, Grace Haven. Jesse's family used to go there too, but his mom and dad recently left and started going to a different church.

Gemma is being extremely quiet, as per usual. Whenever she's around Charlie, she suddenly forgets how to interact. She claims it's because she can't stand him, but I think it's because she has a crush on him.

"Have you guys made any plans for this coming weekend?" Charlie asks, breaking the silence. "We could all go fishing at Camp Willowbrooke."

"Count me in." Jesse says, giving Charlie a fist bump.

Gemma looks up from her french fries and just stares at Charlie. I roll my eyes and visibly cringe. I love her but she can be so embarrassing.

"If my grandparents are cool with it, you can count me in too," I reply.

Jesse reaches over and puts his arm around me. I lay my head down on his shoulder and he presses a kiss to my forehead. I love it when he does that. It makes me feel like I'm the most important thing in this world to him.

"Get a room, lovebirds," Charlie jokes.

"Charlie, I heard you started seeing a girl from Silver Oak Ridge," Jesse retorts, raising an eyebrow. "What's her name again?"

Charlie turns five different shades of red and my sister goes into a coughing fit. Silver Oak is our rivalry school—anytime we play against them in sports, it's always a big deal. Dating a Silver Oak Ridge Tiger? That's just asking for trouble.

"Yeah, but we're just talking. We're not together or anything." Charlie shrugs, trying to downplay the situation.

"Whatever you say, Charlie." Jesse smirks and gives him a knowing look.

Later that weekend, I'm sitting on my grandparents' porch waiting on Jesse and Charlie to pick me up. I was right when I guessed that Gemma didn't want to tag along.

There's a spot not too far away from the campgrounds' entrance where we usually try to fish at. Jesse and Charlie swear it's the only place where a certain breed of fish lives, and it's just become a part of our fishing routine.

Jesse's red truck pulls into the driveway and I get butterflies as soon as I see him. I don't know if they'll ever go away. He's been my best friend for years, but there's just something about him.

I glance down at my outfit—black running shorts, a cheerleading t-shirt, my favorite hat, and tennis shoes. I learned my lesson to never wear flip-flops fishing again because the last time I did, I got poison ivy in between each of my toes. Talk about a nightmare.

I grab my bag and start walking towards him.

When I reach the truck door handle, I notice that Charlie isn't with Jesse yet. Maybe we're picking him up next?

I settle into the middle seat of the truck so I can be as close to Jesse as possible. The familiar scent of the worn seats and Jesse's cologne floods my senses. My stomach dips. As much as I try to act like he doesn't affect me, I can't help the way my body reacts whenever I'm with him.

Jesse looks over at me with that easy smile of his, the kind that makes my heart flutter around in my chest. "Good morning, Cora." He leans in and gently presses his lips against mine. It's a slow and soft kiss that's full of tenderness and love.

When our lips part I swear I can still feel him. I look up at him like he's my entire world because at this moment, he is. "Good morning, sweetheart," I say with a bright smile.

He licks his lips and breaks eye contact first. "I brought you some of your favorite things."

He reaches into the back seat and pulls out two drinks and a white bag with the words 'cream filled donuts' written on it in black ink. I blink at the bag, caught off guard by how well he remembers the little things about me—like the fact that I hate custard filled donuts and prefer cream filled.

"You remembered!" I squeal and take the donuts from him and set our drinks in the cup holders. "There's only two drinks here, is Charlie bringing his own?"

"Charlie had something come up and he couldn't come anymore, so it's just you and me." He takes my hand in his and backs out of the driveway.

My grandparents live about fifteen minutes away from Camp Willowbrooke, so we have some time to listen to music and eat our donuts. Jesse's truck is an older model and doesn't have bluetooth or an aux cord, but it does have a radio and CD player.

I press the play button on the CD player to see what he's been listening to. Bluegrass music from an old gospel band starts to pour out of the speakers and I shake my head and laugh. That's my Jesse, he's such a papaw.

We listen to two or three songs before he stops the music. "Cora, can you reach into the glove compartment and get out the purple CD cover?"

"Sure thing," I reply as I give him a skeptical side eye.

I open the glove compartment and pull out the CD case. My breath catches in my throat—It has 'Coraline's playlist' written on it with a red sharpie.

"Jesse, what is this?" I ask, my voice barely above a whisper. My heart is racing at the speed of a humming bird again.

"I know you get tired of listening to my old school music. So, I made a playlist of your favorite songs so that when we ride together you can listen to your favorite music too."

My mouth drops open and I stare at the CD in awe. That is, without a doubt, the sweetest thing that anyone has ever done for me.

"What's wrong? Do you not like it?" He starts to nervously ramble as we stop at a red light. "I didn't know if it was too cheesy or not—"

I grab his face with my hands and plant a single kiss on his lips.

"That is the most thoughtful thing anyone has ever done for me. Thank you."

I kiss him again and we start to get lost in the kiss. It's more desperate and hungry this time—entirely different from the soft kiss he gave me earlier.

I thread my fingers through his hair and he groans, continuing to kiss me back.

A car horn honks from behind us and I jump at the noise and start to laugh—until I notice that the car that honked was his mother, Keri.

My smile fades and my stomach drops. I break away from Jesse and scoot over to the passenger side seat. Trying to put some space between us.

"Crap," Jesse mutters under his breath as he wipes his mouth.

The light turns green and he turns down the backroad to Camp Willowbrooke. His mom starts to follow us.

"Did you tell her where we were going?" I ask, trying to keep my voice steady.

"Yes, but I didn't get a chance to tell her that Charlie wasn't coming with us anymore."

Her car starts to creep up too close to the truck. She starts honking, urging us to pull over. The donuts that I was savoring earlier now make my stomach church.

"What is she doing?" I ask as I hold onto the handle above the passenger side door, or the 'oh crap handle' as my grandpa calls it.

Jesse glances at me, apologetically. "I don't know, but I think I've got to pull over. I'm so sorry Cora." He puts his blinker on and pulls over to the side of the road.

The air around us that was once full of happiness and excitement, now feels tense.

Before I can even reply, Keri's car screeches to a halt behind us. Her tires screeching against the pavement. She slams her car door shut and the moment she gets out of the car I see it—the wild, crazy look in her eyes. My stomach twists even more.

Jesse unbuckles his seat belt and steps out of the truck, leaving me behind, frozen in place. I don't have the bravery to face whatever is about to happen next. I grip the seat and watch them from the rearview mirror.

I can't tell exactly what's being said, but I've never seen her face that red before. Her veins are standing out in her neck and her arms flail around in anger.

Jesse doesn't speak. He just stands there, on the side of the road, with his head down and his hands in his pockets.

This definitely was not how I pictured today going. I think I can count this date as over.

9
Coraline

Present Day

I'M STANDING IN THE master bathroom of the rental house, double checking my appearance. It's Sunday. We're going to church today for the first time in over a year, and it will be my first time attending service at Grace Haven in seven years.

I know that it's the perfect church for raising a family—I just hope my boys will love it as much as I once did.

I decided to wear a flowy, midi dress. It's my favorite shade of lavender and has a white floral print on it. The sleeves are short and fit loosely, not too tight but also not too big. I paired the dress with a pair of nude pumps.

My strawberry blonde hair is curled in loose waves and pulled half up and half down with a white hair bow. I applied a light pink lip gloss and kept my makeup toned down.

I nervously run my hands down my dress to smooth it out for a third time. I need to go check on the kids and see if they're ready yet. We have to leave in fifteen minutes, and Michael always makes us run a little bit behind. I don't want to get there late today and have even more eyes on us.

I can't help but wonder what everyone will think of me when they see me with my two sons and no wedding ring. Will they think less of me? Will they try to kick me out? Will they know all the things I've done and call me out on it?

I exit the master bedroom and walk across the hallway to the room that the boys are sharing. There are two, twin sized beds on each side of the room—one for Harrison and one for Michael.

Harrison's bed is filled with all of his favorite stuffies and a mountain of pillows.

Michael's bed is more simple. He only has one stuffy on his bed, his favorite teddy that Nash bought for him when he was a baby. My heart squeezes when I notice the bear. Nash may have turned into a monster, but to that little boy he's still his daddy.

The kids aren't in their room, so I walk down the rest of the hallway to the living room.

Harrison is sitting in the recliner watching TV and eating a chocolate chip muffin. Thankfully, he's completely ready.

I inspect his outfit—a new gaming t-shirt, a pair of jeans and a matching pair sneakers. He did an awesome job on picking out his outfit. I've been trying to let him do more for himself so he can develop a sense of independence but I also don't want him to walk around looking like a mad man.

"Good morning bub," I say in a sing-song voice. "How are you?"

"I'm fine," he replies shortly, not looking up from the TV.

"Are you excited to meet some kids your age today?"

"That would be cool I guess," he gives me a small smile.

"Have you seen Michael? I already checked the bedroom."

"Yep," he nods. "He's in the kitchen getting some cereal."

I turn the corner to the kitchen and see Michael sitting on the ground. He's scooping up his favorite cereal that's been spilled all over the kitchen floor.

"I'm sorry mom," he says as he looks up at me with his big brown eyes. "I thought I could get it by myself. I was just hungry. I will clean it up, I promise! Please don't be mad at me."

Guilt stabs me in the chest. Am I mad that he made a mess? No, not even in the least bit. It's literally just cereal.

I recognize that this is something that would have sent Nash into a spiral. He always overreacted over the tiniest things. It got worse this past year, along with his overconsumption of alcohol.

I kneel down on the floor next to him and scoop him into my arms. "Sweetheart, I'm not mad at you. Accidents happen and it's not a big deal. We can buy you some more cereal while we are out today." I press my lips to his cheek and wipe his tears away with my hands.

"Thank you, Mama," he says as he sniffles. I realize that yet again, I made the right decision for my kids and for myself. The mark that Nash has left on us, will never fully go away.

I turn the car into the church parking lot and pull into an unoccupied space. The lot used to be gravel and dirt. It's recently been paved and painted.

Grace Haven looks like a typical small, southern church. It's made out of brick and there's a white steeple with a cross located on top of the building. The windows on the sides of the church walls are made out of blue stained glass.

When I was growing up, the windows were one of my favorite things about the church. When we would go to evening services, the sunlight would filter through the stained glass and cast an array of blue hues. It always felt serene and peaceful.

An aged marquee sign is nestled in the front of the church surrounded by a bed of colorful summer flowers. The church's name, Grace Haven, is painted at the top of the sign, along with Pappy's name as pastor.

I turn my attention to the clock in my car, nine fifty-five. We made it five minutes early. This is a good time to arrive when you want to walk straight in, get a seat and avoid talking to everyone.

I glance around the parking lot to make sure Shae's car is here, and then I shut the car off. She texted me the other day and invited us. She mentioned that their children's program has really grown the past few years, and I know that it will be good for my kids.

I scramble to get myself and Harrison and Michael out of the car while making sure I don't forget anything. I grab both of their hands, and we walk together to the front doors.

Once we enter the building, an overwhelming wave of nostalgia and anticipation washes over me. The church usher, my great uncle, is welcoming everyone as they enter. He notices me and my children, and his face lights up.

"Well, if it isn't Miss Coraline Jennings," he chuckles. "I have missed you more than you could ever imagine. I am so glad to see you!" he says, embracing me in a hug.

"It's nice to see you too, Uncle Timothy." I say, giving him a real smile. His hug and the kindness in his eyes has already made me feel more comfortable.

"Who are these fine men here with you today?"

"This is Harrison, and this is Michael. They're my sons," I reply, my head held high, proud to be their mom.

He shakes both of their hands and pats the top of Michaels head. "It's very nice to meet you two fellas. Are you all taking good care of your mama?"

"Always," Harrison replies.

The sound of a bell starts to chime. Grace Haven still rings the church bell when it's time for service to begin. "We'd better go find a seat," I say while pulling them along with me through the sanctuary doors.

The sanctuary has a middle aisle with rows of pews on each side. The flooring throughout the entire church is still the old original hardwood, and another one of my favorite things about the church. The walls are painted a creamy white, and a few portraits of Jesus are mounted on them.

I start to feel a panicky sensation in my chest when I realize that Shae is sitting all the way up front, three rows back from the first pew. Everyone at Grace Haven is definitely going to notice us now if we sit front and center with her.

I swallow my pride and walk down the aisle to sit with her despite the voice in my head telling me to turn around and run back out the door. Once she sees us, her eyes light up, and she smiles. I sit down on the padded pew next to her and smirk to myself.

"I was afraid that I'd catch on fire when I entered the sanctuary," I whisper to Shae. She rolls her eyes and playfully shakes her head at me.

One of the church deacons approaches the podium, greets everyone, and opens the service with a prayer. I bow my head and pretend to pray along with him.

All of a sudden, goosebumps rise up my arms. I lift my head and look across the aisle. My stomach drops. At this point it feels like Jesse is following me. I went seven years without hearing a single peep from him, and now I feel like he's there every time I turn around.

I notice yet again that he's only gotten more good looking. I was hoping he would be overweight and bald but that's not the case. It's really not fair.

He's wearing a blue-button down shirt with the sleeves rolled up to his muscular forearms. He has on khaki dress pants that fit him perfectly. His blue eyes meet mine and I blush. He totally caught me checking him out.

What's gotten into me? I'm supposed to hate him. He didn't want anything to do with Harrison. I cannot entertain him. I make an effort to keep my head straight ahead the rest of the service, trying to ignore the hole he's staring into me.

The deacon steps away from the podium, and it's time for the choir to sing. Grace Haven still sings out of hymn books that are older than everyone in attendance.

Granna is playing the piano as the congregation sings along with the choir. She messes up on a note but only Pappy catches it— and me, of course. I don't miss the look they give each other and their smiles. It's like they're speaking to each other through their facial expressions alone. I've always wanted a love like theirs. Maybe one day I will have it.

Next, it's time for prayer requests. Every church has its own way of handling them. Grace Haven is old-fashioned and small, so anyone with a request just speaks it out loud, which is incredibly anxiety-inducing for me

Several people request prayer for the sick. I recognize that some of the names mentioned are patients of mine.

"I have an unspoken prayer request."

I refuse to turn my head and look at him. I can physically feel how clammy my palms are and how red my face is getting. I'm starting to get hot, despite it actually being kind of chilly in the sanctuary.

They must've installed a new AC unit over the years, which they desperately needed. Nothing worse than facing conviction and being on the verge of a heatstroke.

After everyone is done praying, it's time for the kids to go out to their classes. They separate the classes by age. Harrison and Michael are in two different groups and once they realize that, they turned around and gave me a nervous glance. I nod reassuringly at them and give a thumbs up.

I'm astonished at the number of children that are in attendance today. I know Shae had mentioned that the program was doing really well but I didn't realize it was this large of a group for such a small church.

My heart swells with pride. I'm so glad that Grace Haven has created this safe space for kids to come together, learn about God, and make friendships that will last a lifetime.

I lean over to Shae and whisper, "Do they still fill all the kids up with cheeseballs?"

"Yes, of course," she whispers back and pats my leg.

Once the kids are in their respective classes, Pappy approaches the podium and begins his sermon. It's the strangest thing because it was exactly what I needed to hear.

It's almost like he looked inside my mind and was preaching right at me, even though I know that's not possible. Pappy knows what I've been going through at home with Nash and the kids, but he had no way of knowing I was coming today.

He preached on forgiving those who have wronged us and letting go of the things of this world that are weighing down our spirits.

I feel a pull so strong to go up to the altar, to pray, and lay down all my burdens, rededicating myself to God. But, my anxiety starts to take control, and I feel like everyone's eyes are on me.

My breathing speeds up, and I feel like the walls are closing in on me.

I can't stand the idea of so many people watching me and judging my every move, especially Jesse. Maybe I'll do it another day—if I come back.

10
Coraline

"How was your Sunday school class?" I ask Michael as I buckle him into his car seat.

"It was so cool! I had so much fun!" He eagerly replies. He has orange cheeseball residue around his mouth, all over his cheeks, and his hands.

I grab a baby wipe from the back seat and let out a small laugh as I clean his face and hands. Then, I shut the door and climb into the driver's seat.

I go to adjust my rearview mirror and see Harrison with an exasperated expression on his face.

"What about you, Harrison? What did you think about church? Did you learn anything?"

"It was fine I guess. There were a couple of kids my age and they were cool. We learned about a dude who was in a dirt hole with hungry lions. The lions didn't eat him because God saved his life."

"Well I'm glad one of you paid attention," I joke. "But I am happy that you both enjoyed it."

I buckle my seatbelt and start the car.

"Mom, can I ask you something?" Harrison says softly.

"Yes, of course sweetheart."

"Why was the man who fixed the oven at church, and why did you guys keep staring at each other?"

"Well..you see...we...I.." I keep stuttering over my words. I knew this day would come, but now that it's here, I don't know what to say to him. I can't lie to him and at the same time I don't want to break his heart with the truth.

"I know you know him, Mom. Please don't be mad at me, but I found a picture on your bed the other day and it was of you and him. You guys looked like boyfriend and girlfriend."

"That was a long time ago sweetheart, let's talk about this later. Why don't we just go to Granna and Pappy's house and get our bellies full first?"

Harrison nods his head in agreement. My grandparents talked to us after church and invited us all to have lunch at their house. Shae is going to tag along— she's basically their granddaughter too. We used to spend so much time together at their house when we were growing up.

I turn on the radio and back out of the parking lot. My heart is hammering in my chest. I feel the urge to cry, but I hold it in. If I cry, he'll be even more suspicious. Maybe I should just go ahead and tell him? I don't know what to do.

"Harrison, can you pass the salt please?" Granna asks.

The boys, myself, Granna, Pappy, and Shae are seated at the worn dining room table in my childhood home. My grandparents have had this table since they first got married in the late 1960s. Even though it's an old house, it has excellent bones and has been well taken care of.

All Granna watches on TV are 'Hallmark' reruns and the 'HGTV' channel, so whenever she sees a new trend, she redecorates.

Her style is one of a kind for her age. She incorporates new things, like modern furniture in the living room, fresh paint colors, and even modern rugs and curtains. But she also keeps sentimental pieces from throughout the years as little Easter eggs in her home.

Growing up, we used to always eat together after church with all my great aunts and uncles here at the house. As the years have gone by, we've lost so many of them. It feels really nice to sit here at this table and enjoy a home-cooked meal that isn't frozen pizza or food sent by an estranged ex-baby daddy.

Granna made beef and noodles, mashed potatoes, green beans, and dinner rolls. It's one of my favorite meals—comfort food. Right now, I can use all the extra comfort carbs I can get. Granna said she had an overwhelming feeling that we would be coming over soon, so she made extra, just in case.

"So," Pappy says as he wipes his mouth with a napkin. "Have you thought any more about the thing we discussed on the phone last week, Coraline?"

I finish chewing my food. "I have, actually. I think it's a great idea. They've never been camping, and I know that I always loved to go with you all when I was their age. We'll go."

"Go where?" Harrison asks.

"Camping in an actual, real life camper at Camp Willowbrooke. It's going to be so much fun! We can all ride bikes together and play at the park. They even have a creek that we can get into and catch some little fish and crawdads."

"Ew! Gross! Crawdads?" he replies with disgust. "Can I bring my video games?"

"No," Pappy replies. "This is an electronic free trip. There will be plenty of things to do outside, in the real world."

"Also, dear, don't forget about the big party that will be going on. Boys, I heard that there's going to be some carnival rides and inflatables to play on," Granna adds.

"Woah! That will be so cool!" Michael cheers. "I can't wait!"

This year marks the one-hundredth anniversary of Camp Willowbrooke. The entire town will be gathering to celebrate. Granna and Pappy had to reserve their campsite a year ago for their camper because the sites were selling out so fast.

I haven't camped in an actual camper at Camp Willowbrooke since I was thirteen or fourteen years old. Their camper is large enough to accommodate eight adults, so having three extra people stay with them won't take up too much room.

The only reason I stopped going with my grandparents was because high school cheerleading was too demanding of my time. I always had summer cheer programs and we practiced multiple times a week to prepare for competition season in the fall.

"Shae, are you going to be able to make it out?" I ask.

"Yes," she replies. "I wasn't able to get a spot reserved, but John and I will for sure come out and spend time with you all and sit around the fire."

"That's perfect!" I turn back to Granna. "Have you heard back from Gemma? Did she decide to go too?"

"She's still thinking about it. She said she will come out and visit with Goose, but she doesn't know if she will be staying."

I can tell that Granna is a little disappointed. It would be just like old times if Gemma decided to stay. We have so many special memories from camping together every year. I can't wait to make new ones this summer with my own children.

11
Coraline

One month ago

THINGS WITH NASH HAVE continued to get worse. His manic drinking episodes used to only happen once a week, never more than twice. This week, it's happened almost everyday. I can't keep living like this.

I took the day off today so I could pack some overnight bags for the kids and take them to my grandparents house. Granna and Pappy are vaguely aware of the situation, but they understand how serious it is—they drove two hours to meet us halfway. The kids think they're going to spend a fun filled weekend with them, which isn't a lie.

I'm just glad that they're oblivious to what's actually going on with Nash. They understand that something weird is going on and that he's been more grouchy, and I've tried my best to hide the worst of everything from them as much as possible. But it's hard to do that when the evidence of his abuse is everywhere. I've lost count of all of the holes he's punched in our bedroom over the past month.

I've been quietly collecting evidence against Nash. I know that I need to have solid evidence before I can even attempt to put him behind bars. He's been too drunk to notice—or care about—anything beyond expecting dinner to be ready when he stumbles in late at night, and me waiting for him in his bed. I don't even call it *our* bed anymore. There's no love left here. Whatever we had is long gone. These past few months have been the darkest, most painful of my entire life.

Even though I want to, I know that I can't just up and leave. If I do that, he will come after me. I'm afraid that if I push him too hard, he will actually kill me or do something to my children. This is the reality that I'm living in. I feel like I'm living a double life. I'm so tired of pretending that I'm okay and like I'm not actually screaming and dying on the inside.

This is really going to happen tonight. There's so many ways that this could go wrong. My anxiety is starting to get the best of me.

When I turn into my driveway, my heart stops. Nash is home. He hasn't come home early in almost a month. It's only four p.m.—maybe he just came home to change before heading back out to whatever bar he frequents. I'll just go inside and play it cool. Odds are, he won't even notice that the kids aren't with me anyways.

I sit in the car for a moment, gripping the steering wheel. Deep breath in and deep breath out. No big deal. I can do this.

I step out of the car and wipe my sweaty palms on my jeans. My hands tremble as I fluff my hair. I flip the mental switch in my mind so I can pretend.

Pretend that I still love him. Pretend like everything is just fine. Pretend like I'm actually someone else. It's the only way I have been able to make it this far. The only way I have been surviving—keeping him from spiraling and falling apart.

The real me though? I hate him, but that doesn't keep me or my children safe. Love—or at-least the false illusion of it—does.

When I walk inside of the house, the first thing that I notice is that all of the lights are off.

Nash is sitting at the kitchen table with his hands folded together, like he's been waiting on me.

His glassy, bloodshot eyes lock onto mine as soon as I approach him. He doesn't do anything, just sits there and glares at me with a look of hatred.

The kitchen reeks of stale liquor and sweat. Nash looks like he hasn't showered in a week—his hair's flat and greasy and he has a five o'clock shadow. He's even still wearing the same dirty clothes from two days ago. The same stained flannel with a hole in the right sleeve. The same gray sweat pants with dirt stains on the knees.

There's a thick and electric tension in the room that hums beneath the surface like the calm before the storm or like a power line that is ready to snap.

"It's about time you came home," he says softly. My heartbeat thunders in my chest. He picks up the bottle of liquor from the table and takes a long swig. "Where were you?"

A simple question, but I have to answer it the way he wants me to or he will lose it.

"I was just out for a drive. I needed to clear my head a little bit. Work has been really stressing me out." I didn't lie to him. I did need to clear my head today and work has been stressful recently.

"Oh really?" He slowly shakes his head, like a bull getting ready to charge. "You see, I think you're hiding something, Coraline." He puts the bottle back down on the table. "I'm going to ask you one more time. Where. Were. You." He spat as he enunciated each word.

"I'm not lying to you baby. I would never do that." I start to walk towards him to attempt to calm him down.

I can see the rage swirling around in his dark brown eyes. I know if I don't calm him down now, it's going to get worse.

Nash picks up the glass liquor bottle, without warning, and hurls it across the room.

It explodes against the kitchen wall with a deafening crack. The brown liquor runs down the wall and starts to pool on the floor. I flinch, but I don't scream. Any sound that I make can make his temper worse.

Slowly—carefully—I slide my hand into back pocket and wrap my fingers around my cellphone.

I hit the button on the side of the phone five times, a trick I recently learned, to call 911 without alerting Nash.

After the fifth time, my phone lightly buzzes once—this confirms that the notification went through.

I try my best to keep my poker face on so he doesn't know what I just did. I can only pray that they will get here as soon as possible.

He slams both hands down on the table and starts to stand up. "I tried to call you at work today. They told me that you never showed up." He starts to pace back and fourth. "I know you are lying to me Coraline. Where have you been? Who is he?" He slurs in an accusatory tone.

"What are you talking about? There is no other man in my life but you baby." I made sure to keep my voice clear and steady. Pretend Cora, you can do this.

I walk closer to him, ignoring every alarm bell in my head.

Every instinct in my body is begging me to turn around and run the other direction, but I can't. Not yet. I can distract him for just a little longer. Just until the police get here.

"WHO IS HE?" Nash roars, his voice cracking from the intensity of his scream.

He grabs the chair up that he was sitting in and slams it against the wall. The wooden legs shatter on impact and the chair lets fall to the ground.

This is not the first time he's accused me of cheating on him. I know with the look that he has in his eyes right now that he wants to hurt me.

I don't really have anywhere to hide in this house that he won't find me, but I'm sure going to try until the police get here. He starts to rush towards me and I turn around and run for my life.

I sprint to the basement door.

My fingers are trembling and I have to fumble around with the lock, but I manage to twist the deadbolt and latch the chain. I know that won't hold him for long, but it will give me time to hide.

I continue to run as fast as I can down the stairs and to the actual basement. My lungs are burning—but I don't stop.

My feet hit the concrete basement floor and I start to search for the best place to hide.

Luckily for me, Nash never comes down here and in the state that he's in, he doesn't know where anything is at anyways.

I hide behind a mountain of storage totes and crouch down as small as I can. I try my best to control my breathing. In through my nose, out through my mouth.

I pull out my phone from my pocket and make sure it's on silent.

There's a loud crash from upstairs. I flinch and almost drop my phone.

I can hear Nash swearing as he tears the house apart. I also hear him the minute he figures out that I'm downstairs and locked him out. He starts banging and beating on the basement door as hard as he can.

Then silence. Nothing.

Until I hear it. My heart drops when I hear the door start to crack and break. I decide to do something that I haven't done in a long time. I pray to God as hard and fast as possible.

"Coraline, I know you're down there. Tell me where you're hiding and I'll take it easy on you this time." My stomach sinks, I know he's lying. I put my hand over my mouth and close my eyes while I try to focus on being as quiet as possible.

I hear him toss the pieces of the broken door down the stairs, his heavy footsteps follow right after.

Nash trips and falls over the debris, causing him to swear even more. His breathing is ragged and uncontrolled.

Three loud knocks from the door upstairs sends a cold wave of panic all over me. My breath hitches in my throat and my stomach drops.

I bite my lip, hard enough to draw blood, so I don't make any noise.

"Is that him Coraline? Is that your little boyfriend looking for you? Maybe I should give him a warm welcome." He throws something again and spits on the ground.

There are three more knocks and I hear him turn around and go back up the stairs. I make myself continue to sit still. I'm hoping and praying that it's the police.

I overhear lots of shouting and commotion but I can't make out what's being said. Then after a few minutes, I hear footsteps descending from the stairs again.

"Police! Is anyone down here?"

"Yes!" I shout as tears start to spill down my face. "I'm over here."

"Please step out, slowly, with your arms above your head. Put any and all weapons on the ground." I do as instructed.

I'm sitting in the police station now, turning in every piece of evidence that I've been hiding over the past few months.

It's all real now—this nightmare is over. I've answered every question I could and gave the policemen all that I had.

My heart feels lighter than it has in years, like a weight I didn't even know I was carrying has been lifted. Knowing he's behind bars? It's the kind of freedom I never thought I'd have.

It turns out that when the police showed up at my house, Nash opened the door, saw them, and *still* wouldn't let them inside. He was so convinced that I was cheating on him, that he wouldn't listen to anyone else.

That's when the argument started. The officers tried to reason with him, but he refused.

He ran through the house, stumbled out the back door, and jumped into his car.

The police immediately followed him and tried their best to get him to pull over.

The chase didn't last long. He crashed before they even got close.

Now, not only is he facing second-degree assault, but the police have added a DUI charge to his record, along with reckless driving and resisting arrest.

I pray I never have to see him ever again.

12
Coraline

Present Day

I'VE SEARCHED HIGH AND low for the kiddie grocery cart with the car on the front of it, for at least ten minutes now. "I'm sorry bub, I don't see it anywhere and we've really got to get started."

"But mommy..." Michael's lower lip starts to tremble. I take his hand in mine, but before I can say a word, he starts to cry. "You promised me that I would get to drive the car inside of the grocery store today."

It's seven p.m. and we've had a very long day. Michael isn't used to being out all day and is exhausted. When he's this worn out and things don't go his way, it's tough for him to manage his big feelings.

"I know baby," I say as I bend down and wrap him in a hug. "We have looked everywhere, but it's just not here today."

That only makes him cry harder. I'm so overstimulated and overwhelmed, I seriously consider just calling it quits and heading home empty-handed. But if I don't push through, it won't get done—and there's barely anything in the kitchen as it is.

"What if I let you get a new toy? Would that make it better?" I offer, in hopes of calming him down.

"No!" Michael crosses his arms over his chest.

An older woman passes by with her cart and chuckles, "I remember those days." She walks off, still laughing to herself.

After another five minutes of negotiating, I finally convince Michael to ride in the normal grocery cart. His only condition is that he gets to play on my phone while we shop.

I didn't really think that through well enough because my grocery list is on my phone. I won't be able to check it while he's on it. But at this point, I can't afford to pick and choose my battles. I guess i'll just wing it.

After going down almost every aisle and allowing Harrison to throw whatever he wanted to get into the cart, I've discovered that I really strayed way from my grocery list. We got way too much stuff.

Of course, with my luck, every person in the entire grocery store goes to check out at the same time I do. Every register has three or four people, all with full grocery carts.

We're going to be here awhile.

The line finally starts moving, but the kids are so restless at this point that I'm not sure I can handle it much longer. Being a single parent is incredibly overwhelming, and on days like this, it feels like I'm drowning in responsibility—like I'm just not good enough.

It's finally our turn to unload our grocery cart and check out when the boys start to fight.

"Boys!" I whisper urgently. "You guys have got to stop it. We're almost done and then we'll be home before you know it."

That lasted all of thirty seconds. I'm completely drained, both physically and emotionally, and I can't even deal with how ridiculous the situation has become. I just give the cashier an apologetic look and mumble an apology.

After the groceries are all bagged, I reach into my purse to get out my wallet.

The cashier tells me my total, and I reach for my debit card—only to realize it's not in my wallet. My stomach sinks. Can this day possibly get any worse?

"I think I left my card in the car. I grabbed fast food earlier and sometimes I get in a hurry and forget to put it back inside of my wallet. I'll be right back!" I explain to the cashier.

I grab both kids and we do the quick, awkward walk of shame to the car, all while praying my debit card is somehow there. We search every inch—underneath the seats, in every compartment—and still, no card.

I take a step back, take a deep breath, and run my hands down my face. I've accepted my fate.

"I think I found it!" Harrison exclaims while holding up my golden debit card.

"Praise the Lord!" I exclaim. I grab both of their hands and we start the trek back into the grocery store.

My heart drops again when I get back to our register. Jesse Cooper is chatting with our cashier and holding a receipt. When he sees me, he gives me a playful grin.

"Excuse me Jesse," I say as I push past him to get to the cashier. "I found my card!"

"He's already paid for it. No worries," the cashier replies.

"He did what?" My blood immediately starts to boil. First the food dump and now this?

"It's really no trouble at all," he says as he crosses his arms and smiles again.

"Can I talk to you in private?"

"I suppose so," he says, following me and the kids back outside and to my car.

I buckle both of the kids inside of the car and turn on some music for them to listen to. My kids and the rest of the grocery store are out of earshot now.

Jesse is making himself right at home and is leaning against my car like he doesn't have a care in the world.

"How dare you?" I sneer.

"How dare I?" he shoots back. "I was just being a friendly neighbor to the new family in town. It really was no trouble. It looked like you had your hands full today and I wanted to help out."

"I am not a charity case Jesse. I have a full time job and I have money. I do not need your help." I cannot believe the nerve of this guy. He wanted nothing to do with his own son for years and now, out of the blue, he wants to be a knight in shining armour. It's too late now. I am not falling for anyone's tricks ever again.

"I don't think you're a charity case Cora."

"Oh really? You go years without contacting us and then one day you show up and buy us food from every place in town and now you're buying us our groceries."

His eyebrows furrow, a mix of anger and confusion crossing his face. "How did you know about the food? It was supposed to be anonymous."

"Your name was printed out on every single bag," I deadpan.

"Look, you weren't supposed to know about the food. I was just trying to cheer you all up. I could tell you all are going through something and I–"

"Well you can stop." I cross my arms. "I don't want you anywhere near me or my kids. You had your opportunity. Now leave us alone."

I turn around and practically jump inside of the car. I have both hands on the steering wheel and I take a few deep breaths to try to calm down.

I go to put the car in reverse so we can finally go back home and I realize that I forgot to unload the groceries and they're still sitting behind the trunk in the cart. Jesse stands there and just stares at me with a blank expression on his face. Why me God?

13
Jesse

I PARK MY TRUCK in Cora's grandparents' driveway and turn off the engine. Something's felt off between us lately, and no matter how hard I try, I can't shake the feeling that something's changed.

I grab the flowers and cookies from the passenger seat and make my way to the front door. We're supposed to start college together in just a few weeks. I'm hoping she's just nervous about that—and not something more. I picked up some of her favorite flowers and cookies, in hopes that they'll cheer her up.

Our entire senior year all we've talked about is our plans for after graduation. There was never a doubt or a second thought in my mind that I was going to leave Scottsdale and go anywhere without Cora.

We've spent so many nights daydreaming about getting married, settling down, and maybe even having a little version of us someday. Just the thought of her becoming my wife still brings a smile to my face. I know I'm young, but deep down, I know—she's the one.

I knock on the front door and wait. I shift the flowers and cookies in my arms.

As the seconds drag on, I start pacing the porch. She's taking longer than usual to answer. With every passing moment, the uneasy feeling in my chest grows stronger.

After a few minutes, she finally opens the door and steps outside with me. That's... unusual. Normally, I'd go right in, say hi to her family, and then we'd slip off to her room or the basement. But not today. Something's different—and I can feel it.

"Hey Cora, I got these for you. They're your favorite." I smile and hold out the flowers and the bag of cookies.

She sniffles, and that's when I really see her. She looks like she's been crying for a while and her eyes are red and puffy.

"What's wrong?" I ask, my voice softening with worry. "Did something happen?"

I reach out to hug her, instinctively wanting to comfort her—but she takes a step back, and the space between us suddenly feels cold.

"Don't. You're going to make this harder than it needs to be."

"Cora, what are you talking about?" I ask, my voice barely above a whisper.

"Jess," she says, her eyes brimming with tears. "I know you have this big picture in your head of our future, all these plans—but over the past few weeks, I've realized something... our dreams just don't match anymore."

My stomach drops and a tightness grips my chest like a vice. The back of my throat starts to burn. I have to swallow, just to keep it together.

"I know you thought everything was great," she says, voice trembling, "but you never really asked me what I wanted. You just told me what you thought I wanted." She takes a shaky breath and wipes at her eyes. "I've been thinking about this a lot the past few days, and I realized that I don't want to stay here for college. I want to see the world, figure out who I am, and chase my own dreams."

"Okay," I say, without missing a beat. "I'll go with you. No big deal."

"Jess," she says softly, shaking her head, "I don't want you to come with me. That's not *your* dream. Your dream is to stay here, close to your family and I think that's beautiful. But it's not what I want anymore."

It feels like the walls are closing in on me, and I can't catch my breath. My hands go numb, and the flowers and cookies slip from my grip, falling to the ground.

"Cora," I choke out, my voice barely steady, "are you breaking up with me?"

"Jesse, I'm so sorry." This time she tries to reach for me and I'm the one who flinches. I can physically feel my heart shattering.

I bend down, pick up the flowers and cookies, and without saying another word, I turn and walk away.

As I head back to my truck, I make a promise to myself—I will never let another woman hold my heart like that again. If this is what heartbreak feels like, I never want to feel it again.

I tossed the flowers I bought for Cora out of the window as I drove home. I thought about throwing the cookies out too, but there was no way I was letting those bad boys go to waste.

When I pull up to my house and get out of the truck, I spot my mom sitting on the back porch. She has a fruity drink in her hand. Her body is turned toward the driveway, like she'd been waiting for me to come back early.

"Jesse! Come here, son," she calls out. "I just got off the phone with Coraline's grandparents—they told me what happened." She sets her drink down on the outdoor table and hurries over to wrap me in an embrace.

"Too soon, Mom," I say, my voice flat and monotone. "I need time to process what just happened. I do appreciate your concern and sympathy, though."

"Oh, nonsense," she says, patting my shoulder as if she's trying to soothe me. "You didn't need that floozy of a girl anyway. You're too good for her. I love you so much." She presses her red-stained lips to my cheek, and I cringe at the gesture.

"Mom, why don't you like Cora?" I ask, the words slipping out before I can stop them.

"Why would I like her?" she snaps, as if it's the most obvious thing in the world. "How could I ever like someone who just wanted to take my baby away from me?"

I walk over and sit down in the chair beside her, my head dropping to her shoulder. "Will the pain ever go away?" I ask quietly.

"Of course it will," she says, her voice softening. "One day, you'll wake up and it'll feel like she never existed."

14
Coraline

I SLAM THE FRONT door behind me and rush to my bedroom.

As soon as I'm inside, I lock the door and crumple to the floor. All you can hear in the room is the ragged sound of my gasps as I struggle to breathe.

My chest heaves. It feels tight and suffocating, like I can't get enough air into my lungs.

My tears are so hot against my skin that it feels like they're burning my cheeks as they streak down my face. Raw, unfiltered agony rips through my chest, crashing over my heart like a tidal wave. This is the worst pain I've ever felt, the kind that makes you question how anything could ever feel whole again. How will I ever recover from this? How can I ever be whole again?

"God, please make it stop. Take the pain away. I can't do it anymore. Please, God." My voice trembles as I whisper the words through my sobs. I pull my knees into my chest, curling into myself on the floor, seeking whatever comfort I can find in the fetal position.

"Can you hear me God?" I cry. "Why does it hurt so bad?" My voice breaks off and my chest shakes with my silent sobs.

I had to break up with Jesse today. It was the hardest thing I've ever done, but I knew it was what was best for both of us.

Last week, his mom, Keri, confronted me, telling me how unhappy I was secretly making him. She said he complained about me all the time behind my back, that I made him miserable, and that I was holding him back from being happy.

She suggested that I needed to let him go, so he could explore new things and find his own happiness again. The more I thought about her words, the more they started to make sense to me.

I know that he's too nice to break my heart and I couldn't bear being the one who made him feel that way, so I let him go.

I knew that if I was going to do it, it had to be like this—no turning back. But the truth is, I still love him, and that makes it hurt so much more. Letting go doesn't make the pain stop. It just makes it more real.

I keep imagining him with someone new—taking her to our spot, kissing her, holding her hand, loving her the way he once loved me.

The weight of my newfound loneliness crushes me, and I clutch my hands over my chest, trying to hold myself together. Another sob breaks through, silent but sharp, and it rips through me, leaving my throat raw.

Every happy memory flashes through my mind like a movie—when he asked me to be his girlfriend, our first kiss, our last kiss. Every laugh, every shared moment of joy. It all plays over and over in my mind, too vivid to ignore. That's all I can think about, and it's both beautiful and heartbreaking at the same time.

After what feels like hours of crying, I finally stop.

I sit up, feeling completely drained, like there's nothing left in me.

Slowly, I push myself off the floor and climb into bed. I open my laptop, hoping to distract myself. I scroll through my email and remember that just a few hours ago, I applied to a college in the city.

It's called the Maple Grove Institute, and the campus looks like something out of a fall romance novel. It's a few hours away from here. Maybe a new beginning is exactly what my heart needs. I've got to do this, not just for him, but for me too. If letting him go is what it takes for him to be happy, maybe I can find my *own* happiness again.

15
Coraline

FRESHMAN YEAR AT THE Maple Grove Institute, this will be the best year yet. I just know it. I get out of the car and take a deep breath in and inhale the smell of the crisp, fall air.

Fall is my favorite time of year. It's not too hot but also not too cold. You get to dress in cute sweaters and go to fall festivals and pumpkin patches. It's also football season.

This will be my first year since I was four years old that I won't be supporting a football team from the sidelines. Instead, I will be supporting them from the stands like everybody else. It's one of the few things, besides school dances, that I feel like I already miss. I loved cheerleading so much.

Jesse was the quarterback at our high school and I was the head cheerleader. We were always together and he was my best friend. We really were something straight out of a movie.

Living a life without Jesse has felt impossible lately, considering I just broke up with him three weeks ago. He's my first and only love. He was my first everything but I had to leave. I don't ever want to be the reason someone is miserable with their life.

Scottsdale will always be home to me. Maybe I'll go back one day, but my new adventure starts now. I need a change. That's why I picked Maple Grove. It's four hours away and right smack dab in the city.

Like a typical freshman, I have on my Maple Grove t-shirt and matching hat. I have my hair pulled back into a ponytail and I put on a full face of makeup.

I want to make a good first impression in this city. Everyone in Scottsdale knows me as Jesse's girlfriend. I want to be known for being me this time.

The atmosphere feels so alive here. Families and students are unloading their cars and moving into their dorms. This will be my new home for the next four years and I'm full of butterflies and excitement.

I turn to my grandfather and give him a hug. "Thank you, Pappy. I'm going to miss you but I promise to call every evening." I feel him take a deep breath and wipe at his eyes.

Pappy is dressed in his typical papaw attire; dress pants, a button down with a pocket and dress shoes. His white and gray hair is combed to the side and his reading glasses are tucked into his shirt pocket with his handkerchief.

"I love you Coraline. Make smart choices." Pappy takes out a small, square piece of fabric. "Make sure to keep this with you."

I look down at his hand and see a prayer quilt. It's a four inch by four inch square made out of quilted fabric with a bible verse in the middle of it that has been anointed. He places it in my hand and hugs me one last time.

"I will Pappy," I squeeze him harder. "I love you too."

Two weeks later

I feel something cold on my face. I try to open my eyes and realize that I'm laying on the tile floor in my dorm bathroom. I'm wearing the same outfit I had on last night. Everything is too bright and my head feels like it's about to split open. What happened?

I sluggishly push myself up into a sitting position and pull my legs to my chest. I've never felt this sick in my entire life. I've been feeling queasy the past few days, all day long, but this is the worst it's ever been.

The entire room feels like it's spinning in one big circle. My stomach starts to churn and my mouth begins to water. I'm definitely going to throw up again.

My eyes start to burn with unshed tears and a sob threatens to tear its way out of my throat. I wish my grandparents were here to help me. I miss them so much.

I don't know how long I've been in here. I can't believe how careless I've been.

At this point I don't think I can even keep my head up. I know I need to go to the hospital, but how am I going to get there? My family is four hours away and I haven't made that many friends yet.

Last night was all one big blur. The last thing I remember was playing a drinking game at a fraternity house with my roommate. I can't recall anything that happened after that. She promised to take care of me if something ever happened and I promised her the same.

I crawl out of the bathroom on my hands and knees and move to my tiny, cot size bed. Our dorm room is small but it has been completely updated as of two years ago— so, at least it's not outdated and small.

Sleep. I need to sleep. If I can just get into my bed and sleep I will feel better. I reach over to my nightstand, grab the prayer quilt that my grandpa gave me and hold it to my chest. I mutter a quick prayer that I will feel better soon.

I need to find my phone. I've got to call someone to take me to the hospital. I start to pull myself up so I can get into the bed when my stomach churns again. This time I really am going to throw up. I grab the closest thing I can reach and empty my stomach contents.

I lay my head back down and everything fades to black again.

16
Coraline

WHEN I WAKE UP, the first thing I notice is the sharp smell of bleach and disinfectant. My whole body feels like it's been hit by a truck. I'm so tired.

As soon as I open my eyes, I wish I hadn't. My grandparents and my sister are here with me. They're all wearing looks of disappointment and worry.

"What happened?" I mutter softly. "How did I get here? How long have I been asleep?"

I look down and notice that there's an IV in my hand and I'm hooked up to what feels like a hundred monitors. Someone has changed me into a hospital gown and my clothes are nowhere in sight.

"It seems that you passed out in your dorm room and your roommate called an ambulance," Granna replied. "Sweetheart, we've been so worried about you." She stands up and moves her chair so she can be right beside of me. "I knew something was going on after you stopped calling to check in." She reaches for my hand and places it in hers.

"I'm so sorry," I say as I start to tear up. Pappy won't even make eye contact with me. What have I done? I feel so ashamed.

I've always, for the most part, been a rule follower. I never did anything crazy in high school. I was always home on time. I never snuck out. I went to church every Sunday. I was a straight A-B student and never got into any trouble.

I think the break up with Jesse and trying to navigate life on my own has started to lead me down the wrong path. I attended one on campus church event and never returned because I started going to parties with my roommate.

I only started going out because I wanted to make some new friends and my roommate was very persuasive. The first time I ever got drunk was at a party with her and I liked the way it made me feel. Drinking made me forget about Jesse. It made me feel invincible.

There were three soft taps at the door. "Miss Jennings, may I come in? My name is Dr. Jamison."

"Yes, you can come in."

Dr. Jamison is a middle aged doctor who looks like he's the star of a medical TV show. His black hair is pushed back and styled perfectly. He's wearing navy scrubs and I also notice that he has a gold chain around his neck with a cross on it. He's holding a clipboard and has a tight expression on his face.

"Miss Jennings, is it okay if we talk about some of the medical tests we ran while you were asleep in front of your family? It's completely up to you." He asks as he starts flipping through some of the paper on the clipboard.

How is this guy old enough to be a doctor? He's so handsome and he smells good. I feel like I'm in a fever dream.

"Yes, of course," I reply, nonchalantly.

"Miss Jennings, I'm not sure how to say this so I'll just be blunt. Did you know that you're pregnant?"

My ears start to ring and I start to see black spots everywhere. Everything starts to move in slow motion. The only noise in the room is the alarm going off on one of the monitors.

"Pregnant?!" My Granna gasps and covers her mouth with her hands. She turns to look at me with a sad expression on her face.

Pappy's face turns as white as a ghost and he's staring straight down at his feet.

"No sir, there's no way I'm pregnant. Dr. Jamison, I think you all have made a big mistake." I start to laugh nervously. I know I have been partying and drinking but I haven't slept with anyone. I knew that for sure. Didn't I?

"Maybe the test got mixed up?" I suggest.

Dr. Jamison walks over to one of the monitors and silences the alarm. He looks at me with piercingly blue eyes. "According to your HCG levels in your blood you're about eight weeks along. There's no way it got mixed up. They actually ran it twice to be sure."

My heart drops, eight weeks.

Eight weeks along.

The only person I've ever been with is Jesse. I haven't been with Jesse since we broke up. I start to hyperventilate and I feel a panic attack coming on. What am I going to do?

"I know this is a lot of information to take in at once, but there are lots of options. If you would like to discuss or look into them, I will leave a few packets that have resources on them for you to review."

He sits the packets of paper down on the bedside table and pats my shoulder. The he gives me a tight, uncomfortable smile and exits the room.

The tension in the room is so thick that I don't even think a knife could cut it.

17
Coraline

I'VE BEEN STAYING OFF campus at my grandparents house since I got discharged from the hospital.

The ride home was the most uncomfortable car ride I have ever experienced. I was an ugly mess, Granna was hysterical and Pappy was eerily quiet. Poor Gemma is probably traumatized for life now.

Bringing a baby into my life right now feels absolutely insane. I looked at all of the resources that Dr. Jamison gave me and I feel like abortion is not an option for me.

I made certain choices and now I am paying for my actions. I know that I had my mind dead set on leaving this town to keep Jesse happy—but now I know for sure that God has other plans for me and for this baby.

I've tried to contact Jesse multiple times now. The first time that he finally answered me, he told me to never contact him again and hung up.

I texted him after and told him that it was incredibly important and that I needed to speak to him ASAP. He then proceeded to block me— he also blocked me on every social media profile that he had.

I get that he's mad at me, but if he would just let me explain the situation I know he would put aside how he feels for me and focus on the baby.

I don't expect him to take me back, that's not why I'm contacting him. I just want him to have a chance to be the good dad that I know he has always wanted to be.

The morning sickness, not a hangover as I had once thought, has been tolerable today. Whoever named it morning sickness is a liar because I have been sick all day long. I can't believe I didn't connect the dots sooner.

I'm sitting in my childhood room and I have my prayer quilt clutched in my hand. My eyes and throat start to burn. I wish Jesse would answer me.

As a last resort effort, I decide that I'm going to have to call his parents. I'll tell them since he is still refusing to talk to me. Maybe they will understand since it's their grandchild.

I take a deep breath and pull out my cell phone.

I open up his parents home phone number and dial it. Someone answers on the first ring.

"Coraline, I think it's pretty clear that Jesse does not want to talk to you." Keri's high pitched voice rings through my speaker. I cringe and move the phone away from my ear.

I've never gotten along with Jesse's mom. She's an acquired taste of a woman and is too overprotective of her son. I tried to win her over multiple times but eventually gave up. It wasn't worth it. I learned that there is no pleasing her or making her happy.

"Mrs. Cooper, I know that I have made mistakes and I wish I could go back in time and change them, but that's not why I'm calling," I say, trying to ease myself into the conversation. I can already tell this isn't going to go well.

"Then what do you want? Quite frankly I don't want to hear from you or your family ever again either," Keri huffs.

I stay silent for a few seconds as I try to think of the best way to do this. I better just get it over with.

"I'm pregnant Mrs. Cooper and Jesse is the father. I've been trying to contact him so I could tell him myself."

"Look, I don't know why you think you're having a baby with my son but he's right, you're actually crazy. We have all heard about how wild you've been out there in the city. I bet you don't even know who the dad really is. My Jesse will not be your saving grace. Do not contact us again."

She hung up the phone before I could even formulate a response. I'm stunned. My mouth actually drops open. I can't believe she just said that to me.

She's the one who told me that I needed to leave him. She confessed that he told her I was bringing him down and making him unhappy. I'm starting to think she lied to me about him. I'm mad at myself for even entertaining her lies.

There is no question that Jesse is the father. I've never been with anyone else. I don't know how else to get in touch with him without showing up at his doorstep, which sounds like a terrible idea after what his mother just said to me. So, I pull out a sheet of paper, grab a pen and write everything down.

I say a prayer to the man up above and mail the letter. The ball is in his court now. There is only so much I can do to make him hear me out. I have to accept it and make peace with it.

18
Jesse

IT'S FRIDAY NIGHT AND the crew and I are hanging out in the garage after a long week. I laugh to myself because the "crew" isn't really a crew at all—it's just me, Charlie, and John.

They're the only two people, besides my parents, who know about the software I sold and the money that came with it. I don't have to hide anything from them.

The garage is basically our man cave. It's decked out with a pool table, ping pong table, and a small kitchen with a bar. But the real highlight is the flatscreen TV I mounted last year. It's perfect for watching football and basketball games with the guys.

Over the years, I've collected various vintage metal signs from all the places I've traveled to on vacation. I've mounted them on the garage walls for décor, and honestly, that's about as far as I've gone with decorating.

It's nothing fancy, just a perfect escape from everything. When we're in here, it's like the outside world doesn't exist—just good games, good friends, and no distractions.

I open the fridge and pull out a cold, cherry soda. I scuff my work boots on the concrete floor, fix my hat, and pop the top off of the glass bottle. "Do you guys want a cold one?"

It's always been a running joke to "crack open a cold one" at my place, but I don't drink alcohol. I don't judge anyone who does, but alcoholism runs in my family, and I've seen firsthand how it can tear someone apart when abused. Charlie and John know this and respect my decision, which I appreciate.

"I'll take one!" Charlie says, raising his hand as he lounges on the futon, flipping through TV channels.

"What about you, John?" I ask, glancing over at him.

"I'll pass this time. I'm trying to watch my summer bod," he replies with a laugh, patting his stomach.

John's not a big guy by any means, so his comment made me chuckle. "Yeah, right. By the way, I already ordered a pizza for us. I got your favorite, John," I wink at him.

John leans back on the couch, letting out a sigh. "Honestly, after the day I've had, it'll be a miracle if I can eat anything."

"What kind of trouble did you get into today?" Charlie teases.

"I was hoping you'd ask," John says, sitting up a bit. "If you really want to know, I was at Henry and Mira's farm doing an emergency delivery of a calf."

John's a pro when it comes to emergency situations like that. He's the best emergency vet in Scottsdale—and the only one.

"Remind me not to shake his hand," Charlie whispers to me, his face twisted in a playful look of disgust.

"You're such a wimp, Charlie," John says, rolling his eyes but laughing. "I guess when they left for their vacation, they had no idea one of their cows was pregnant. She was in labor for who knows how long. It's a miracle that both of them were okay after delivery."

The whole thing sounds like another one of John's crazy adventures, but he never lets it phase him. I can't even imagine the stress he must've been under, but he's always calm in those situations.

Lucy, my German Shepherd, took that as the perfect time to greet Charlie and John. She trots over to them and lets them him pet her, one at a time.

"Come here, pretty girl," I call out.

Lucy runs over to me and flips onto her back. I rub her belly and her head lolls to the side with her tongue sticking out. She really is the best companion ever. She's spoiled plum rotten too.

I sit back on the bar stool and take a swig of my pop. "How's life in paradise with Shae, John?"

"Honestly, things are going pretty good. We're still planning on tying the knot soon. She's been busy with wedding planning, and I've been busy delivering baby cows." We all laugh.

"Shae told me about Coraline moving back into town." He pauses and looks at me while smirking.

"Is that so?" I ask, avoiding eye contact.

"She also told me that you bought food from every restaurant in town and had it delivered to her house."

I cringe and I can feel my face turn tomato red. I look down at my drink. "I ordered the food online. She wasn't supposed to know who it came from."

"Are you trying to get back into her good graces?" Charlie prods.

I shrug, still not looking up from my drink. "I don't know, man. It wasn't about that. It was just... I figured it might help, you know? She's going through a lot right now, and I didn't want her to feel alone. I hate seeing people unhappy, especially kids."

John leans back, giving me that typical half-smile of his. "I get it. You're trying to be a good guy. But if you're not careful, you might just end up complicating things even more."

"No. I moved on from her years ago," I roll my eyes hoping that they don't see straight through me. "I just felt bad about her oven breaking and decided to do my neighborly duty and welcome her back into town."

"Whatever you say, Jesse." John snickers.

"Charlie, how about you? How's your love life going?" I try not to poke too much into Charlie's love life because I know he is still holding on to his grief.

He tried to go on a date one time earlier this year and Jenny, his daughter, found out. She had an absolute melt down. She was only three when her mother passed away and I can't even begin to imagine how hard it is for them.

All I can do is be there for them and pray that God will send him a wife that will help pick up his broken pieces and love him unconditionally.

"I'm still not ready to try, not with what happened the last time."

I nod in understanding and leave it at that.

I'm sitting on my front porch swing with Lucy, her head resting gently in my lap as she gazes up at me with that familiar look of adoration. It's a lazy Saturday evening, and I couldn't ask for a better way to wind down.

This morning, my dad and I got up early and took the boat out on the lake. We each caught four fish, making it a pretty successful day of fishing at Camp Willowbrooke.

After fishing, I met up with the camp staff to continue working on ideas and plans for the 100th year celebration. We ordered the materials that were requested and assigned roles to everyone.

We've got an excellent lineup of food trucks and local vendors, plus plenty of activities for the kids. I made sure to carve out a spot for Pamela from the Scottsdale Diner and her famous banana pudding cake—no celebration would be complete without it.

We have a few local singers and gospel bands lined up to play for everyone. It should be a really great time for the town to get together and enjoy the campground. Cora's grandfather is supposed to be in attendance to kick off the celebration and bless the party with a prayer.

Speaking of Cora, my gaze shifts toward the rental house where she's staying. To my surprise, I spot her sitting on her back porch, enjoying the evening just like me. I watch her for a moment, trying to study her from this distance with the sun setting behind her. A part of me wonders if I should go over and talk to her.

I'm not angry at her anymore. I've let go of the past. I gave it to God. I've moved on from everything that happened between us years ago, but I can tell she hasn't. Every act of kindness I've offered has only seemed to make her more upset.

I want her to let go of whatever lingering resentment she's holding onto. I need her to see that I'm a man now. I'm not that high school football star anymore, and I'm definitely not the same little boy she left behind. I can handle whatever comes my way.

I bow my head and say a small prayer, asking for God's guidance.

"Well, Lucy, looks like I'm doing it. Wish me luck girl," I say while pressing a gentle kiss to her head.

19
Coraline

IT'S OFFICIAL—I'VE JUST HAD one of the worst days ever. I haven't had a day this bad since I was in nurse practitioner school, juggling a toddler, a newborn, and all the chaos that came with Nash.

I worked overtime at the clinic yesterday, then had to pick the boys up from my grandparents' house once I was done. By the time I grabbed fast food, got them home, bathed, and tucked into bed, it was already ten o'clock.

It seems silly, but I hadn't been on my phone at all yesterday other than to call Granna and let her know I was working over. When I finally had time to check my phone, I had four missed calls from Nash.

The first voicemail was from the *nice* version of Nash—the one wrapped in his fake charm he shows to everyone else. He told me how much he missed me, how beautiful I was, and how he couldn't wait to see me and Michael. He didn't mention Harrison at all.

But then, the voicemails started to shift—each one more bitter, more venomous than the last. He threatened to call CPS, to have my kids taken from me. He made sure I knew just how much he hated me.

The last one shattered me. He called me a terrible mother, and accused me of neglecting my kids and sleeping around with multiple men. That was the one that finally brought tears to my eyes. I wasn't just mad at him—I was furious at myself, for not seeing through him sooner.

I was so full of hurt and anger, all I could do was lie in bed and cry. I tossed and turned all night, unable to relax. Sleep came in short, restless bursts—maybe a few hours at most.

When I finally got up this morning, I glanced at my phone and saw a text from my sister, Gemma. She asked if the boys wanted to come over and stay the night.

She mentioned that the boys could play with her dog, Goose. As soon as I told them, they were sold.

Goose is like a giant, golden teddy bear, and he absolutely soaks up all the attention Harrison and Michael give him.

Honestly, I think a sleepover is a perfect idea. Right now, I'm not in the best headspace to give my kids the best version of me. And as much as I hate admitting that, it's true. You can't pour from an empty cup—and mine is just about empty.

I'm twenty-five years old, a full time nurse practitioner and a single mom with two boys under the age of ten. Why do I constantly feel like I'm not doing enough? Like I'm not good enough?

I just can't shake this overwhelming pressure to pull myself together. It's like a knot in my chest that won't come loose. So here I am, sitting on the edge of the porch with my head in my hands, listening to the quiet hum of the evening. Everything feels still around me, but inside, it's chaos.

A thought crosses my mind that maybe I should be praying about my situation like I used to do. My prayer quilt is inside of the house. I could get up and go get it.

I'm just so aggravated right now, I push the thought aside. I don't have the emotional energy for that right now.

I'm lost in my thoughts when a faint rustling sound cuts through the stillness.

Out here, this close to the campground, you never really know what you're going to see. We get all kinds of wildlife—deer, coyotes, even the occasional bear. I've always been afraid of them.

The rustling sound gets closer and my head jerks up instinctively.

Jesse Cooper is walking onto the property, heading straight toward me. My stomach drops. He must have the stealth of a cat because I didn't notice him until he was practically on top of me.

If this was a scary movie, I'd already be dead.

I roll my eyes. Why can't he just stay away? With the kind of day I've had, I think I would've preferred the bear. I am *not* in the mood for this tonight.

"Can I help you?" I huff, while crossing my arms tightly over my chest. I don't know why he insists on showing up at the most inconvenient times. Does he not get it?

His brow furrows, and his eyes narrow slightly. "Cora, will you hear me out? Then, I swear, I'll leave you alone for good this time." He leans against the tree in my backyard, folding his muscular arms across his chest. His posture is calm, but there's an edge to his voice that makes my pulse quicken. "We're going to be around each other in this town, whether you like it or not. We might as well talk through whatever's bothering you."

He's dressed in typical Jesse attire—jeans, work boots, and a form-fitted t-shirt that hugs his muscles in all the right ways. How can I be so mad at a man and still notice how good he looks?

I hate how effortlessly he carries his confidence, it's the kind that always made me second-guess my own feelings. It's not fair. I'm supposed to be angry, but all I can do is watch him, unable to tear my gaze away.

"Jesse, how did you even get here?" I throw my hands up in the air.

"What did I do to make you hate me so much? What grudge are you still holding on to?" He pleads. "If you're mad at me for buying your groceries, I do apologize for not getting your consent first. I genuinely do things like this to help lift people's spirits. Not because I thought you didn't have any money. I would never do anything to embarrass you."

"You are exhausting," I say while I close my eyes and shake my head. "It's not that."

"Then what is it?" He asks.

The last thing I want to do right now is engage with him, but it's too late to back down. Maybe I'll feel better if i get this off of my chest.

"When you blocked me, I understood. We were young and foolish, and I had just broken your heart. But when I told your mom about Harrison, and she flat-out told me I was lying, I realized something. I thought the Jesse I once loved would want to step up and be there, to be a father. When you didn't, it crushed me." I bite my lip, suddenly feeling exposed, vulnerable. "I didn't want to raise him without you, Jesse. But I couldn't make you care."

"Wait," he interrupted, his voice a mix of confusion and disbelief. "A what?"

I glare at him, placing my hands on my hips. "Really, Jess?"

"Coraline, I'm dead serious. What are you trying to say?"

"You don't know?" I ask flatly, my voice heavy with disbelief.

"Know what, Coraline?" His confusion deepens, and I can see the tension building in his expression.

The words hang in the air like a heavy fog, and I can feel the weight of them between us. "You're Harrison's father. I tried to tell you, but you refused to speak to me. After your mom threatened me, I mailed you a letter explaining everything. When you never replied, I took that as my answer."

His face pales, and for a moment, he seems to freeze in place. Then, his voice cracks with a tremor, the tension between us palpable. "Does Harrison know?"

"I think he's starting to suspect," I reply honestly. "He found an old picture of us in my room and started to ask me questions. I was always honest with him about the fact that Nash was not his real dad. He never asked about who his real dad actually is."

"My mom knows." I see Jesse's expression shift, a mix of confusion and pain crossing his face. "And she never told me?" His voice is quiet, but there's an edge to it, like he's trying to make sense of everything.

I stand there, feeling a rush of emotions I wasn't prepared for. All the anger I had been carrying for years, the bitterness, the resentment—it all vanished in less than a minute. I realize, with a sinking feeling, that he truly had no idea about Harrison.

"I need time to think," he says, his voice distant, as he continues to stare off into space. "Can I contact you once I've had time to process everything?"

I just nod, not trusting my voice right now.

I take his phone in my hand and type in my number.

"If you'll excuse me Cora, I have a place I need to go." He turns around and starts speed walking towards the house on the lake.

"Jesse! Wait up!" I reply and take off after him.

Jesse doesn't stop walking, but I can see the tension in his shoulders. I catch up to him and take a breath, trying to steady myself.

"You're in no state of mind to go anywhere right now," I say, catching my breath. "Why don't you come sit on my porch? I'll get you something to drink and I'll call Charlie or John to come and get you so you're not alone."

He pauses but doesn't turn to face me. For a long moment, we both stand there, the air between us heavy with unspoken words. Finally, he exhales sharply, his hands clenching at his sides. He looks up at the sky, then back at me, his voice quiet.

"I'll take you up on that," he says, his words barely above a whisper. "Thanks."

We walk up onto the porch, and Jesse takes a seat, sitting ramrod straight in one of the chairs. He places his hands on his knees, but I notice the slight tremor in them—an obvious sign that his anxiety is through the roof. His legs start bouncing rapidly, unable to keep still.

"I'll be right back," I say, stepping off the porch and heading inside to grab him a glass of sweet tea. As soon as I'm out of earshot, I pull out my cell phone and dial Charlie's number. He answers on the second ring.

"Hello, this is Charlie." Charlie's voice is warm, familiar, and a little curious.

"Charlie, are you busy right now?"

"Coraline?" He says, confused.

"I wouldn't be calling you like this if it wasn't important. There seems to be a huge misunderstanding that I'll let Jesse go into detail about, but basically..." I take a deep breath and exhale, trying to steady myself. "Jesse is Harrison's father. I thought he knew about it and had purposely abandoned him."

I pause for a moment, collecting my thoughts. "He came over to my house to confront me, and it came up in the discussion. He said he has someplace he needs to be, and I don't feel comfortable with him being alone right now or driving anywhere. I think he's in shock."

There's a long silence on the line. It feels like forever, but in reality, it's probably just a few seconds.

"I was on my way to my parents' house to pick up Jenny," Charlie finally says, his tone steady but with a hint of concern. "I'll turn around and head your way now."

"Thank you, Charlie." I exhale a sigh of relief. "Do you know where my house is?"

"Of course I do. It's right beside his." Charlie hangs up, and my heart skips a beat.

The beautiful house I stare at every day is his.

20
Jesse

That was the last thing I ever expected to come out of Cora's mouth. The fact that she thought I knew all this time blows my mind. I try to process it, but it feels like everything is unraveling too fast for me to catch up.

The first time I laid eyes on Harrison, I do remember feeling like he looked familiar. At that time, I thought maybe he just looked like a young Cora. I never, in a million years, thought he could be my son. How could I have missed that? The signs were right there, and I was too blind to see them.

My stomach twists painfully, and the churning feeling intensifies. A cold sweat breaks out across my skin, and I suddenly feel weak, like the ground beneath me is ready to give way. I try to steady myself, but it's like everything in my life is spinning out of control.

For years, I've been living the life of a single bachelor, completely oblivious to the fact that I have a son out there. A son who's been through God knows what.

I squeeze my eyes shut, trying to block out the whirlwind of thoughts and scenarios that keep popping into my head. If I let myself go there, I might really lose it. I can't even think about it right now. The guilt, the confusion, the regret—it all feels like it's suffocating me. I've got to get up and move.

I hear movement in the field between our houses and glance up. My heart skips a beat when I see Lucy sprinting towards me. She's running full speed, her fur ruffling in the wind as she moves. When she reaches me, she jumps up and starts licking my face, her warm, familiar presence grounding me in that moment. She somehow knew that I needed her. She is my steady shadow in the middle of all this chaos.

That's when I realize I've been crying and Lucy is licking my tears away. I need her right now more than ever. It's like everything I once knew has shifted beneath my feet, and now I'm standing in a life that doesn't quite feel like mine.

"You're such a good girl Lucy." I rub her favorite spot behind her ear.

After a few minutes pass and I've had time to calm down, I sit back down in the porch chair and let out a long, shaky breath. Lucy settles at my feet, her head resting on my boot. I can tell she's not going to let me out of her sight willingly again.

I reach down and run my fingers through her fur, grounding myself with the steady rhythm. The back door opens and Cora steps back outside with a glass in her hand.

"I called Charlie. He said he's on his way." She holds the glass filled with amber liquid out to me.

I nod in acknowledgment and take it from her. I take a sip and instantly recognize the familiar taste of sweet tea—my favorite, especially in the summer. I'm too upset to even enjoy it.

If Cora thought it was odd that a large dog is at her house, she doesn't say a word about it. But I did catch the small, almost reluctant smile she gave Lucy.

"When you've had time to think it over and make a decision, maybe we could get dinner and talk—really talk. I'll answer any questions you have, no holding back. If you decide you want to be part of his life, we'll figure it out together. We'll make a plan that works for all of us. I won't fight you anymore," she says.

We're both sniffling now, wiping at our eyes between shallow breaths. There's a heaviness in the air, but also a sense that maybe we're not standing on opposite sides anymore.

The sun has finally set. The only light now, aside from the full moon hanging heavy in the sky, is the soft, amber glow of the string lights draped across the porch. Of course it would be a full moon. That would be just my luck. It should be beautiful—peaceful, even—but tonight it feels like an omen.

Then I hear it—the crunch of tires on gravel. My anxiety spikes. Charlie.

Without a word, I stand and start speed walking toward the headlights that I know belong to his truck.

"Jesse, wait! What do you want me to do with your dog? I assume this is your dog anyways."

"She'll go back home when she's ready. She knows the way. Maybe she will keep you company, unless she's bothering you?" I say, without turning around.

I open the truck door and climb inside, shutting it with a little more force than necessary. My hands tremble in my lap as I take several deep breaths.

"Take me to my parents' house, please," I say, my voice barely above a whisper.

Charlie glances over at me, concern etched across his face. "Are you sure you want to do this right now?"

"There's no sense in waiting. I won't be able to sleep until I confront my mom."

Charlie nods silently and puts the truck into reverse.

I feel completely out of control—like I'm a passenger in my own body. This isn't me. And that only makes me angrier.

What would our lives look like now if I had called Cora back? Would I have married her like I always planned to? Would Harrison be growing up in a stable home, with both his parents by his side?

And the worst part—the part that makes my stomach twist—who else knew? Who else has been keeping this from me, intentionally?

My throat burns when I start to think about my own mothers betrayal and from all of the things that I've missed out on with Harrison.

Why me God? Why is this the path I'm being put on? I've been a good and faithful man. I go to church every Sunday. I pray daily. I volunteer at the church and for this town whenever I can. Why do I feel like I've done something terribly wrong and that this is my punishment?

I glance in the rearview mirror and catch a glimpse of Cora gently petting Lucy. If I wasn't so hurt right now, I'd probably be able to admire her even more than I already do. She's always had this quiet strength about her—something I didn't fully appreciate until now.

I can't imagine how hard it must've been. Eighteen, pregnant, and completely alone while I was here, living my life freely without a second thought—without judgment, without consequences. She carried all of that weight while I was blissfully ignorant.

If I were her, I would've hated me too.

When we turn onto the driveway, Charlie eases the truck to a stop. The tires crunch over the gravel as he shifts it into park. I glance at the dashboard— nine p.m. A little late for a surprise visit, sure, but not late enough to change my mind. I meant what I said—I won't sleep until this is done.

From the window, I catch a shadow moving in the living room. It's my dad. He's probably dozing in the recliner, half-watching the news like he does every night. A pang of guilt hits me, but it's fleeting. My focus is on the truth now, and the woman who kept it from me.

I unbuckle my seatbelt and push the door open. My feet hit the driveway as I step out, ready to face the answers I've been denied for far too long.

I don't have a plan—just a fire in my chest and a name on my lips. I'm going to walk into the house and confront my mom. My fists clench in my lap. I don't even know what I'm going to say to my her. There's no version of this conversation that doesn't end in pain. But the truth deserves to be confronted—especially when it's been hidden for this long.

"I'll stay out here. I don't want to intrude on this," Charlie says, his voice low and steady.

"Roger that," I mutter, reaching into my pocket for my keys. I'm glad I've made a habit of taking them with my anytime I leave my house now.

I climb the steps to the porch and knock loudly on the metal front door. "Dad?" I say as I open the door. "It's me, Jesse."

I don't want my dad grabbing his shotgun and mistaking me for someone who doesn't belong. We don't take kindly to intruders or unannounced visitors in Scottsdale. Especially at this hour.

My dad is sitting in his recliner, reading his Bible under the soft glow of the lamp beside him. I was partially right about what he'd be doing.

He glances up when he sees me. "Come on inside, son. Are you alright?"

"Where's Mom?" I ask, trying to steady my voice and mask the tightness in my chest.

"She's in bed, probably asleep. Why?" His brow furrows as he closes the Bible, marking his page with one finger.

I hesitate, then finally ask, "Did you know?"

He tilts his head, his expression shifting into full confusion. "Know what?"

"Did you know about my son?" I blurt out, my voice louder than I intended.

Dad just stares at me, wide-eyed and silent, like I've just spoken in a foreign language. His expression is somewhere between confusion and disbelief.

Out of the corner of my eye, I catch movement—Mom is creeping down the hallway, tying her robe around her.

Dad crosses his arms, slowly and deliberately. "Jesse... are you high?"

"No, he doesn't know," my mom says softly, stepping fully into the room.

I turn to face her, the weight of everything crashing down on me. "So it is true," I say, my voice cracking. "How could you, Mom?" The words feel like ash in my mouth. "Why would you keep this from me?"

Dad turns sharply toward her, "What is he talking about? What did you do, Keri?"

"Jesse," she begins, avoiding my father's gaze completely. "You have to understand, I was protecting you. I still am. You know how she was when she left town. She was a mess—I never believed that my perfect little boy could be caught up in all of her lies. She never loved you. She was just after your money."

"Stop," I cut her off, my voice sharp. "I don't care what you thought you were doing—there's not one thing you can say that makes what you did okay." I take a deep breath, fighting to keep my composure. "Regardless of what you think of Cora, she told the truth. And I am his father."

"She is trash, Jesse. White trash!" My mom's voice cracks as she throws her hands up in frustration. "She was only going to ruin your life. You need to get away from her while you still can. The day she broke your heart was one of the *happiest* days of my life because you were finally away from her. You could spend more time with me. You're my little boy, Jesse. I love you so much. Can't you see that? She doesn't love you more than me. I was all you ever needed."

I stare at her, my mind racing. "First off, I'm not a little boy anymore, I'm a man. I can and will make my own decisions, especially when it comes to my love life. And mom, I still love Coraline. I always have, and I always will. You cannot change that. And how dare you say that one of the worst days of *my* life was one of *your* best. That's horrible, and honestly, kind of weird."

I pause, the words coming out sharper than I intend. "What about your grandson? Is he not important to you? His life could have been completely different if you hadn't taken it upon yourself to decide what happens in my life."

My heart pounds in my chest as I wait for her response, wondering if anything I just said will even get through to her.

"That child is no grandson of mine," she states, locking eyes with me. My mind races, trying to process what she's just said. Who says something like that? The words hit me like a punch in the gut, leaving me breathless for a moment.

I try to steady myself, but the anger bubbles up, a deep well of frustration and betrayal I didn't even know I had. "What did you just say?" I ask, my voice barely above a whisper, yet it feels like the room is filled with the weight of it.

Her expression doesn't soften. She looks at me like I've just said something outrageous, something she's already judged. "You heard me," she repeats, almost nonchalantly.

I stand there, my heart pounding in my chest. How could she be so cold?

Keri's expression falters for a moment, but only briefly. My dad's voice, stern and sharp, cuts through the tension in the room. It's like a momentary crack in her façade, but she quickly masks it again.

She looks at my father, then back at me, her eyes narrowing. "I'm doing what's best for him. You should be thanking me." Her voice, however, lacks the conviction it had before. It's softer now, but still laced with a chilling sense of control.

"Look," I say interrupting her, "Coraline and I created a life. Whether or not it was wrong of us to do, it happened. You took away my choice of being a father to that little boy for the first part of his childhood. He has gone his whole life without knowing who his father really is because of you." I look down at the ground. "Cora mentioned that she wrote a letter to me. Did you read it?"

"I did," she admits. "I knew there was always a chance that you could find out. I was just hoping I would already be dead by the time it happened."

The words hit me like a punch to the gut, and I stagger back as if the air had been knocked out of me. "You *hoped* you'd be dead before this happened?" My voice trembles, barely able to wrap my head around the coldness of her admission.

I try to steady myself, feeling a cold sweat break out across my skin. She, my own mother, had hoped she'd be gone before I ever had a chance to find out the truth. Before I could ever have a chance to know my son, to have the chance to be the father I should have been.

I take a deep breath and grit my teeth. "You can't just *hope* away the truth, mom. And you can't take away the fact that Harrison is my son." My words are shaking with anger and hurt. "I won't let you or anyone else stop me from being the man I should have been from the start."

Her eyes widen slightly, but she doesn't speak right away. My father, still silent, is looking between us, his expression a mixture of disbelief and regret.

She reaches into her house coat and pulls out a faded envelope, her fingers trembling slightly as she holds it up to me. "I'm not sorry, Jesse," she says, her voice steady but cold. "I still think you need to stay away from her. She isn't good enough for you, and she's going to turn out just like her no-good parents and ruin you." Her words are sharp, like knives cutting through the already fragile air.

She pauses for a moment, as if to let the weight of her words sink in before continuing. "Besides, I heard about her little boyfriend that's in jail. Who's to say she's not just as toxic as him? She will be your downfall, Jesse. She's nothing but trouble, and if you're smart, you'll cut her out of your life before she drags you down too."

The room feels like it's closing in around me as her words hang heavy in the air. Each sentence is a fresh cut, and I'm already bleeding from the last one. I can't even fathom how she could say these things about Cora—about the woman I love—without even knowing her or the struggles she's faced.

I look at the envelope in her hand and then back at her, my fists clenching at my sides. "This isn't your decision to make, mom. It never was." My voice is low, trembling with anger and pain. "I'm not going to listen to you anymore. You don't get to control my life, especially not when it comes to my son."

"I've heard quite enough, Keri," my dad says, his voice trembling with anger. I can feel the raw emotion pouring off of him, his body shaking with fury. "I think you need to leave."

"Oh, come on now, Lloyd..." she protests, but her words lack conviction.

"I mean it, Keri," he snaps, his voice sharp and commanding. She flinches, a flicker of fear crossing her face for the first time in years. It's the first time I've ever seen him this way. "Leave," he adds, his voice colder now. "Now!"

The words hang in the air, and for a brief moment, everything falls silent. There's a weight to his tone that makes it clear there's no room for negotiation. My mother hesitates, her eyes darting between me and my dad, but she doesn't argue further. The finality in his voice has cut through whatever resistance she had left.

My mom turns on her heel and storms off to the bedroom, slamming the door behind her with a force that echoes through the house. The sound reverberates in the quiet room, making the weight of the situation hit harder.

I start pacing back and forth across their living room, my mind spinning. The letter in my hand feels heavier by the second, its presence only heightening the anxiety building inside me.

I glance at my dad, who's still sitting in his chair, completely stunned. He's in shock, just like I was less than half an hour ago. I can see it in his eyes.

To my knowledge, my parents have never had a fight this big. I can't imagine how he's feeling right now.

As much as I want to comfort him, I can't shake the growing sense of betrayal. She's my mom, and I've always held onto the idea that family is everything, but this... this is something I can't just let slide. What she's done, the lies she's told, the way she's manipulated us both—it's unforgivable.

My anxiety is making it hard to breathe. I know she's my mom, but right now, I don't see her as that woman who once cared for me. How do you come back from something like this? How do you redeem yourself when you've taken away my chance to be a father? To be there for my son?

I don't know what happens next, but I know one thing: She's dead to me. There's no turning back from this.

After a few minutes my mom finally emerges from the bedroom and her eyes look wild, like she's lost whatever grip she had on reality. I hear the jangle of her car keys as she grabs them off the counter, and with one swift motion, she grabs a large overnight bag and storms out of the house, not uttering a single word. The door slams behind her with a finality that leaves the room cold.

"Excuse me," my dad says in a hushed tone, his voice carrying a weight of emotion that still hasn't fully settled. He walks out of the room, and I nod, giving him space. He needs it, and so do I.

I sit down on the couch, the letter still heavy in my hand. I finally allow myself to look at it. The envelope is worn, the edges frayed from years of neglect and handling. The faded texture and color of the paper tell the story of time passing—too much time. I can see where my mom must've torn it apart to open it.

The envelope is addressed to me, written in Cora's familiar handwriting. My heart thuds painfully in my chest. The return address is from her grandparents' house, a place I've been to countless times during our relationship.

I exhale a shaky breath as I carefully pull the paper from inside.

I begin to read, knowing that this letter, this moment, will change everything.

"Jess,

I realize that you don't want to talk to me. I understand that I hurt you, and I apologize for that. All I ask is that you hear me out.

I was in the emergency department a few days ago and they did a blood pregnancy test. The doctor told me that I'm eight weeks pregnant. You're the only person I have ever been with and it adds up to the night out by the lake that we shared together.

The doctor gave me a packet of information with different options to explore, since this is an unplanned pregnancy.

I have prayed about my decision. I am going to have this baby and keep it. You're going to be a father Jess.

Can you put our differences aside and make a decision to be a part of our baby's life? I know that in my heart and soul that you will be an excellent father.

Please contact me with your decision.

Also, your mom told me that I was making you unhappy and that you were just too nice to break up with me. She told me that I was doing nothing but holding you back. I listened to her and that is the only reason I left. I want you to know that I regret it everyday.

I'm so very sorry.

With all of my love,

Cora"

21
Coraline

I CALLED SHAE AND told her what happened as soon as Charlie and Jesse left my house. She told me she'd be here in five. In Shae language, that actually means she'll be here in about thirty minutes. I love her to death, but she'll be late for her own funeral.

As I sit in the quiet of my house, the weight of everything that just happened starts to settle in. The tension, the hurt—it's like a storm inside me, and I don't know how to make sense of it all. But even through the chaos, I hold onto something I've always believed: God puts us through certain situations for a reason. I may not know the reason right now, or even how it'll all unfold, but I trust that there's always a purpose.

I choose to trust in God again. I know it'll only make me stronger. No one in this life wants to feel pain. As humans we don't want to feel like we are lost or broken. But, sometimes the worst pain creates the most strength.

I hear the familiar sound of Shae's car pulling into the driveway, the engine sputtering a bit as she parks. I half-smile to myself, grateful for her, no matter how late she is.

As soon as I see her, it's like the dam finally breaks. I can't hold it together anymore. The tears just start to fall, one after another, and there's no stopping them. I've been holding everything in, trying to be strong. But right now, I just can't.

Shae doesn't say anything at first. She just moves towards me, pulling me into a tight embrace. Her hands begin to gently pet my head, pushing my hair back from my face. I squeeze her back, holding onto her like she's the only thing keeping me from falling apart completely.

"I love you," she says softly, and I can feel the sincerity of her words in every fiber of her being. It's exactly what I need right now, even if I can't find the words to say it back. I just hold on tighter, letting the comfort of her presence calm me, if only for a moment.

"You're not alone." Shae's words bring a small, shaky laugh from me as she presses a kiss to the top of my head.

"I don't know what I did to deserve your friendship, but I'm so thankful."

After a few moments, I manage to catch my breath, the tears finally slowing down. I feel drained but strangely lighter, as if part of the weight has been lifted. We head inside to the kitchen, where Shae begins to unpack the bags she's brought with her.

She pulls out a few plastic bags and lays them on the kitchen table. "I brought all of the essentials; your favorite ice cream, popcorn, a chick-flick to watch, fuzzy socks, and face masks. We're way overdue for a girls' night."

I can't help but smile through the lingering sadness. Shae knows exactly what I need. A distraction, some comfort, and most importantly, the reassurance that no matter how hard life gets, I have people who care. Tonight, it might not fix everything, but it'll give me a chance to breathe.

The movie that Shae put on was one of my all-time favorites, *The Princess Diaries*. There's something about a good early 2000's romcom that always lifts my spirits.

We're both sprawled out on my bed, wearing comfy clothes, face masks, and fuzzy socks. I can already feel myself starting to relax.

I forgot how much I need moments like this—time with my best friend, just focusing on each other and not the kids.

Don't get me wrong, I love my children more than anything, but every once in a while, it's nice to take a break and recharge.

When Shae and I used to go to the movies together as teenagers, I'd always add some kind of chocolate candy to the bag of popcorn. She remembered that little detail about me, and made sure to bring a selection of candies for me to choose from, just like old times.

"This is exactly what I needed," I say, taking another bite of chocolate. "It's been entirely too long."

"Agreed," Shae responds, a smile in her voice.

We sit in comfortable silence for the next few minutes, enjoying the movie and our snacks, until it's time to remove our face masks.

"So, how are things going with you?" I ask, my curiosity piqued. "Are you and John still house shopping, or have you all made a decision?"

"John already has his house on his farm, and I think he's really attached to it. It's beautiful, and he worked really hard for it. I think I'm going to agree to move into it when we get married—under one condition," Shae says with a grin.

"What's that?" I prod, intrigued.

"I get to redecorate the entire house, and I get to be a stay-at-home mom," she says eagerly, practically bouncing with excitement.

"What did he say to that?" I ask, trying not to laugh.

"He said yes!" she exclaims, a proud smile spreading across her face.

"Shae, that's awesome!" I say, genuinely happy for her.

Being a stay-at-home mom on a farm is a full-time job that not everyone gets to do. I know she'll be excellent at it.

"When are you all wanting to try to have a baby? If you don't mind me asking. I can't wait to be an auntie, and Gemma isn't showing anything promising at the moment with her dating life." We both giggle at the thought.

"We'll see, I'm not one hundred percent sure," she answers honestly, her eyes glinting with excitement but also uncertainty.

We settle back into the cozy blankets, the flickering glow of the TV filling the room as we watch the rest of the movie. Before I know it, both of us drift off to sleep, the weight of the past couple of days lifting, just a little, as we find comfort in each other's company.

Shae went home about an hour ago so she could get ready for church. She invited me to go back with her again, but what if Jesse is there? What if the boys notice Jesse and start asking more questions that I'm not ready to answer yet?

I just feel so guilty for the way that I've been treating him. I hope and pray that if he decides to have a relationship with Harrison that he will find room in his heart for Michael too.

The thought of Jesse being there brings a swirl of anxiety. I know I can't avoid the situation forever, but I'm still trying to figure out how to move forward with it all. Maybe today isn't the right time to go, maybe I need to just take it slow. Or maybe going to church today is exactly what I need to help clear my mind.

I look down at the prayer quilt in my hand and take a deep breath. I felt so much peace when I came to Grace Haven last week. No one said anything negative toward me or my children. Just smiles, handshakes, and even a few hugs.

I keep having thoughts about all of the reasons I don't want to go. If I stayed home, I would have time to deep clean the house before having to go back to work tomorrow. Maybe I could watch another movie, or start a new tv show. I could finish unpacking the rest of our stuff, and I could even catch up on laundry before the kids come home.

If I choose to go, my kids would be happy to see me. Gemma is bringing them and she mentioned going out to lunch after service, so I would get to eat and spend time with her and my grandparents. Or, I could just stay home in the clothes that I had on yesterday. I could lay on the couch, read a book, and have someone bring me a meal back to eat.

After going back and forth with the pros and cons in my head, I decide to go. The only downside is that I took too long to decide and now I only have ten minutes to get ready.

I ram sack my closet and settle on a sage green, knee length dress with tiny white flowers on it. I pair the dress with a pair of tan sandals.

I pull my long, reddish blonde hair into a low bun with a white scrunchie. I latch my pearl necklace around my neck that Granna gifted me as a nursing school graduation present. They say diamonds are a girl's best friend but for me, pearls are.

I run into the kitchen, grab my iced coffee, and run out the door.

When I walk through the church doors, I see Great Uncle Timothy again. He's dressed in a light green button-down shirt paired with a white tie. His gray dress pants are held up by suspenders, and he looks like a cute papaw. I can't help but smile at his warm, inviting presence.

"Good morning, Miss Coraline," he says with a friendly grin.

I take his outstretched hand and shake it. "Good morning! We match!" I point back and forth between my own outfit and his, both of us in shades of green. He chuckles softly.

"Well, I'll be darned," he says, his eyes twinkling. "I suppose I did pick out the right shirt today after all." He gives me a playful wink, and I feel a little bit lighter.

"Looks like it!" I reply, my nervousness easing just a little. I'm still uncertain about what I'm going to face today, but Uncle Timothy's kind smile helps calm my racing thoughts.

I continue walking and go through the doors to the sanctuary. I didn't have too much time to mingle today because I came in at the same time as the rush.

I try to let the familiar, peaceful feeling of the God's house wash over me. Maybe today will be the step I need to take—whatever happens, I'm glad to have a moment of peace, at least for now. I miss feeling like this.

I look up and spot Harrisons dark curls and Michaels blond hair next to an overwhelmed Gemma. Shae is sitting next to them.

"It looks like you survived another day with my children," I joke.

"I love your little gremlins, but I am exhausted."

Gemma says she's exhausted but she still looks like *Elle Woods* with a face full of flawless makeup. I still need to find out what setting spray she uses.

I greet both boys and sit down in between them. They each grab one of my hands. My heart squeezes so tight it feels like it will burst.

"We missed you mama," Michael whispers in my ear. The weight of his words settle in my heart like a soft blanket.

"I missed you guys too." I smile as Michael leans in, his small, warm hand wrapped around mine. They are such sweet little boys.

It's moments like these that make everything feel right, even when the world around me is chaotic. The love and simplicity in their voices remind me that, no matter what happens, they'll always be my anchor. For now, it's just me and them, and that's all I need.

Church service at Grace Haven starts out the same way as it did last time. We sing old songs out of the worn hymnal books, and everyone greets those who sit around them with a smile and a handshake.

I unintentionally keep looking around for Jesse, but I don't see him anywhere. I feel a twinge of disappointment, which was odd because before I came today I was dreading seeing him. Now that he's not here, I kind of wish he was.

Prayer time comes and goes and then the kids go out to their classes.

Each service before the pastor comes to the podium, the person who leads service offers up time for a testimony. Anyone who wants to give one has a moment to share what God has done for them. It isn't something that you have to do, but it's something that most people enjoy doing. Most of the time it ends with more than half of the congregation covered in goosebumps and sniffling.

"Brother Timothy, I'd like to stand up today and thank God for keeping his hand upon me this weekend." I recognize her immediately. She was one of the patients I was with after hours at the clinic Friday. Edith Clearwater.

Edith is an elderly woman who is very active for her age. She's dressed in black dress pants, a pink button down and a matching blazer. She has a large brooch pinned on her blazer and her white and brown hair is pulled back into a french twist.

"I was working out in my garden Friday evening when I noticed that I was having some trouble breathing. I shook it off as indigestion and continued to work."

The doors to the sanctuary open and I spot Jesse sneaking in. He's wearing the same outfit from last night. His hair is an unruly mess and his eyes are red rimmed.

"I started to feel lightheaded. I figured I was just getting overheated so I took a break and sipped on some water. I kept having a repetitive thought in my head that was telling me that I needed to go to the Scottsdale Clinic."

"I remembered that someone recommended a new doctor in town so I had my husband drive me there. The new doctor ended up being our pastor's granddaughter, Coraline, who is a nurse practitioner." She turns her head in my direction and gives me a small smile. I can feel my cheeks blush from the attention.

"As soon as I got put into a room at the clinic, I started to have an intense pain in my stomach. The pain moved from my stomach and up to my chest and jaw. Coraline wasted no time. She recognized immediately that something was very wrong. I think that God sent me to Coraline for her to save my life."

"She sat there with me until the ambulance arrived, even though I knew that it was past time for her to leave. She made sure I was put into the right hands to receive the care that I needed."

"I am so thankful that she intervened when she did, because when I arrived at the hospital they took me straight back to surgery. I ended up having a stent placed in my heart." She took a deep, shaky breath and continued. "I was having a heart attack and if God had not sent me to Coraline I would be dead." I wiped a tear from my own eye.

"I am grateful for God's guidance and mercy. I just wanted to share with all of you how great He truly is." There were a few "amens" and people were clapping as she sat back down.

Jesse was staring at me with a look of awe and was that adoration in his eyes? My cheeks heat again and my stomach dips.

Would it be wrong for me to allow myself to have feelings for him again since I know that he didn't know about our son? The attraction has always been there. It never went away. But my anger stood in front of my heart and my judgement.

I know I need to work on myself and my family first before I can even think about allowing someone into my heart. I let myself fall for Nash and look at how that turned out.

22
Coraline

I REAPPLY MY LIPSTICK and fluff my hair. Tonight is the first time that I've been on a date since Harrison was born. My grandparents drove all the way from Scottsdale to stay at my apartment for the evening and watch him.

I'm wearing a tight, red dress that hugs all of my curves. I curled my hair in loose waves and went all out with my makeup. I did a smoky eye look with a touch of glitter and I even put on false lashes. I haven't worn false lashes since my high school prom. It feels like stepping into a different version of myself, one I almost forgot existed.

A loud honk echoes from the driveway, interrupting my thoughts.

"That must be him!" I exclaim, grabbing my purse. It feels nice to leave the house without a diaper bag for once. "Thank you guys so much for coming so I could go out tonight. I really do appreciate it."

Pappy raises an eyebrow. "How do you know that's him? Is he not going to come to the door and say hello?"

I stifle a laugh and roll my eyes. "He texted me a few minutes ago and said he was almost here and I know that that's his car."

Pappy shakes his head. "Hmph. In my day, a man came to the door and walked his woman out to the car and opened doors for her."

"Yeah, well," I say with a grin, "welcome to the twenty-first century, Pappy."

I give both of my grandparents a hug and kiss Harrison on the cheek. "I love you baby. I will see you later."

"Bye bye, Mama!" Harrison waves at me until I shut the door.

I walk down the steps of my apartment building and approach Nash's car with my heart beating loudly in my chest. I reach for the handle and go to open the door but realize it's still locked.

I peer in the window and notice that he's glued to his phone. I lightly tap on the glass, trying not to startle him.

He glances up, sees me, and hits the unlock button once. The front passenger door is still locked. It only unlocked his door.

I knock again, this time a little harder, and point to the passenger-side lock. With a dramatic roll of his eyes, he hits the button again, finally unlocking the door for me.

I met Nash a few weeks ago during a six a.m. coffee run. I was stopping at a gas station to get a little pre-shift caffeine and he was in line behind me.

He struck up a conversation and mentioned that he was headed to work at the local coal plant. Then he complimented my scrub top—my favorite one with little dogs on it. That earned him some instant brownie points. I've always had a soft spot for anyone who loves animals.

I told him I was gearing up for shift one of three at the local hospital and that I'd be graduating from nursing school at the end of the month. He congratulated me with a charming smile and asked for my number before I left.

We talked on and off for a few weeks and I made sure to tell him that I was a single mom. He told me that he didn't see any problem with that at all. He even commended me for being such a hard working mother. Two days ago, he finally asked me out on a real date.

"Sorry about that. I was checking on something," he mutters, barely glancing up.

"Oh, that's no problem," I reply with a nervous laugh while tucking a loose strand of hair behind my ear.

"You look really pretty," he said, leaning over to kiss my cheek. The gesture caught me off guard.

Before I could respond, he reached into the back seat. "I got these for you."

He hands me a bouquet of red roses.

"Thank you! That's so thoughtful." My face warms as I smile down at the roses. "You don't look so bad yourself," I add, trying to flirt back as casually as I can manage. I feel so out of place and awkward.

Nash gives a small smirk but doesn't say anything. He's about five foot eight with blond hair, has a well-groomed beard, and has the warmest brown eyes that I've ever seen.

He's wearing a salmon pink polo shirt and khaki shorts, and he smells amazing—like he splurged on one of those expensive colognes that they advertise in TV commercials.

He takes my hand in his and then pulls out of the driveway. My heart starts to beat like crazy again. I've never held anyone's hand that wasn't Jesse and it feels really nice.

Nash wanted to keep the destination of our date a surprise so I don't know where he's taking me. I don't really think I care where we go because I've been so excited for this date.

After about twenty minutes, we pull into a parking lot. "Alright, we're here. Are you ready, beautiful?"

"Yes! Let's go," I say enthusiastically, my voice a little too eager.

I start to pull my hand away, but he stops me. He lifts my hand to his lips and kisses the top of it. Then he looks up at me with those warm brown eyes and gives me a small, almost shy smile.

My cheeks heat and my stomach dips with anticipation.

He gets out of the car first, and I wait—half-expecting, half-hoping—for him to come around and open my door. But after a few long seconds, it becomes clear he's not going to.

I look out the window at him and notice that he's on his phone again. I roll my eyes, grab my purse, and step out of the car on my own.

When I reach his side again, he casually slips an arm around me, like we've been together forever.

"So, where are we?" I ask, trying to get his attention again.

"We are at the coolest bar in town. This is the best place to go and hang out. Have you been here before?" He asks enthusiastically.

I immediately start to break out into a nervous sweat. "No, I uh, I have not."

I don't want to upset him by letting him know that this was probably the worst place to take me. I don't drink alcohol and I've never been inside of a bar before. If my grandparents find out that they drove three to four hours for me to drink at a bar with a man that I barely know, they will be so disappointed in me.

I roll over in bed and stretch, letting out a sigh. The sun is just beginning to filter through the curtains. I slept great last night.

I start to sit up and my foot brushes against something.

I freeze and my heart stutters in my chest.

I jerk upright, swallowing a scream as my eyes dart around the unfamiliar room.

Oh no.

Memories crash into me all at once—blurry flashes of the bar, the drinks, Nash's hand in mine, and then... this. I must have spent the night with him but I don't really remember.

Panic tightens in my chest. I had no intention of staying out all night. I was supposed to head back to my apartment after the date.

I clutch the sheets, nausea creeping in. I've never spent a night away from Harrison. Not once. He sleeps with me every single night. What if he woke up and noticed that I wasn't there? What if he's scared and looking for me?

I need to go. Now.

I quietly put on my clothes and shoes, and I take a peak at Nash to make sure he's still asleep. Thankfully he is. I close the door and make a run for it.

I walk into the hallway of the building and pull out my phone. My gut clenches in dread. I have multiple missed calls and text messages from my grandparents.

I call for an Uber to my location. I don't even know where I'm at or how far from home I am. How did I get myself into this situation again? Am I that desperate?

I feel so much shame and guilt when I step into the elevator in the same dress from last night. I have never in my entire life done something so reckless.

As exhilarating as it was, I just want to go home to my baby. I can never let that happen again.

23
Jesse

I'M RELAXING IN THE kitchen, drinking a cup of coffee. Lucy's sitting at my feet, gazing up at me with big ol' puppy dog eyes. The past forty eight hours of my life have completely uprooted and changed me.

I've gotten on my knees, prayed and cried for God to help guide me as I make a decision that will forever change my life. I know that there is no possible way that I would ever knowingly abandon a child. Especially my own child. I know that I want to be a part of Harrison's life. I just don't know if he will accept me.

I don't really know anything about the kid other than he looks a little bit like me and likes to play video games. Every time I've laid my eyes on him, he just glares at me. And then there's all of the conflicted feelings that I have about his mother.

I've never loved another woman the way that I love Coraline. Sure, we were young when we fell in love, but that doesn't mean it wasn't real. We were best friends in middle school and started dating in high school. You hear the term puppy love in young kids but I loved her unconditionally, with my entire heart. That's why I was so broken when she left me.

My mind keeps drifting back to that letter from the other night, and each time, I get angrier. The frustration builds up again, like I'm reliving it all over. My mom has literally ruined my life because she has some sick obsession with me. I'm mad at myself for not putting the bigger picture together sooner.

I tried moving on, but every time I went on a date, Cora always crossed my mind, and without realizing it, I'd start comparing everyone to her. It's like I couldn't help myself.

I've tried to creep on her social media pages, hoping to find something that would help me understand her and the kids better. But after searching her name on social media for a third time, I remember that I still have her blocked. I should probably fix that first.

After I unblocked her on everything, I quickly learned that all of her accounts are private and I'm too nervous to send her a request right now, so I'll just continue to creep.

On one of her pages I found a picture of her and the kids standing with a man. Someone had posted the picture and tagged them in it. The man in the picture is blond with brown eyes. That must be Michael's dad, Nash.

I click on his profile. His picture is of him and Michael posing for a selfie. Michael is cheesing with a big ol grin and Nash just looks constipated.

His cover photo is a picture of Cora, Michael and him. Harrison was very obviously cropped out. Anger starts to rise up in me again. The fact that he publicly made a difference between the kids raises even more questions about this guy's integrity.

I pull out my cell phone and send a text to Cora.

> Hey, this is Jesse. If you're free, can I call you?

Within two minutes my phone starts to vibrate with an incoming call.

"Hello, this is Jesse."

"Hey Jess, it's me, Coraline."

"Hi, Cora. So, I've been thinking about what you said the other day. I'd like to meet up, grab a bite to eat, and talk in person about my decision."

My leg starts bouncing, and I spill some coffee on the table. Lucy looks up at me, tilting her head sideways.

"That sounds great. I'm at work right now, but can you meet me at the Scottsdale Diner tonight at seven?"

"I'll see you there," I reply, hanging up the phone.

I'm sitting in my favorite booth when the door chimes. Coraline walks in through the door and my breath catches in my chest. I still can't believe one person can be this beautiful.

She's wearing a pink sundress and her hair is pulled back into a ponytail. She scans the room, and when her eyes find mine, they light up. I wave her over to my table.

"Thank you for coming."

"No problem," she replies, offering a small smile.

"Have you said anything to him?" I ask, pushing a little.

"No, not yet. I was waiting for you to make a decision first." She slides her purse off her shoulder and settles into the booth across from me.

I take a deep breath, clearing my throat. "I want to be a part of his life, Cora. As much as he'll allow me to."

She nods, her expression softening. "That's great. I'm so relieved. I'll talk to him and let you know what he says. After that, we can figure out a time for you two to officially meet."

"Thank you, Cora," I say, my voice a little strained as I fight the burning sensation in the back of my throat. My chest tightens and I grab my leg, trying to stop it from bouncing too hard.

"It's the least I can do," she replies, her voice gentle.

I nod, pretending to focus on the menu in front of me. We settle into a quiet, comfortable silence as we wait for someone to take our order. Pamela had already gone home for the day so it was one of the newer staff members who took our drink order.

"So, do you have any questions about anything?" Cora asks, folding her hands neatly on the table.

"Only about a million," I reply, joking. "What does Harrison like to do? I know he's into video games. Does he play any sports?"

"He loves games, but he's not into sports. I've always hoped that one of my boys would get into football so I could watch the cheerleaders," she says with a shrug. "But Harrison hasn't shown much interest. Neither has Michael."

"What does he like to eat?"

"He's all about pizza and chicken nuggets. He's a very picky eater, I think he takes that after you."

That gets a real smile out of me. "Can I see some pictures of him?"

"Of course," she replies. Cora pulls out her phone and opens an album filled with pictures of Harrison, from his birth to now.

"Can you airdrop some of these to me?" I ask, my voice thick as tears blur my vision.

"Yes, no problem," she says quietly, tapping away at her phone.

"This may not be my place to ask, but how did Michael's dad treat them?" I say, my gaze dropping to my hands.

"Oh, I guess it sorta is your place to know these things now, considering the situation," she replies, taking a sip of her pop. "Nash was a good dad to Michael, but he never treated Harrison the same way, and it was obvious. I don't know what you've heard or haven't heard, but he's in jail. I helped put him there. I'm not with him, and I never will be again. He had a drinking problem, and he did things to me that he never should have. But... he didn't do any physical harm to the boys."

I'm speechless, a rush of red-hot anger floods through me. I close my eyes and take a few steadying breaths. I'll never understand how anyone could treat someone like Cora so badly. I don't understand how anyone could hurt an innocent child, even if it wasn't physical. Sometimes the things that other people say stick with you for a lifetime, no matter how old you are.

"How did you all meet? How did..."

"How did I end up with a monster?" She finishes for me, her voice quiet. "They say even the devil is a beautiful deceiver. Nash was very good at acting. He showed one side to the world, the side he wanted everyone to see, and the other side... well, that's who he really was. When I met him, I was young. I just wanted someone to love me, and I walked right into his trap." She pauses, her gaze drifting off for a moment.

"Nash was the first person who ever showed interest in me since I became a mom," she continues, her voice soft but steady. "There were hundreds of red flags that I flat-out ignored because it felt nice just to have someone's attention."

"I was with him for less than a year when I let him talk me into getting pregnant with Michael. We were never married, and he was incredibly controlling—sneaky, too. He wanted all the perks of being a husband without the commitment, and I let that happen. I regret it now. But, I'm putting it all behind me. My focus is on bettering myself and giving my kids the life they deserve."

"Cora, I'm so sorry," I say, the weight of my regret heavy in my chest. "I should have been there for you back then. I should have returned your calls. If I could go back and change it, I would. But we can't change the past, and you're here now. You came back to Scottsdale for a fresh start, so maybe we can have a fresh start too? Put all our differences aside?"

"I think I'd like that," she says, offering a soft, genuine smile.

We continue making small talk for the rest of dinner. I choose not to bring up anything more about Nash or their relationship, even though I really, really want to. Instead, I focus on learning everything I can about Harrison. I jot down all the little details in the notes app on my phone, storing away facts about him for the future.

"I do have a few questions of my own for you Jesse."

"Okay, go ahead." I lean back in the booth and raise an eyebrow.

"The first one is kind of an invasive question, but I need to clear the air." She clears her throat, "When you confronted your mom, what happened?"

I give her a quick rundown of everything that went down at my parents' house, explaining what my mom had admitted. I tell her about finally reading the letter she'd kept hidden all this time, and how my mom had kept my dad in the dark.

"I don't think either one of us would be comfortable with my mother in the picture," I continue, "Would you be open to my dad meeting the kids one day?"

"I've always liked your dad Jess. I think as long as he's truly as innocent as you believe him to be, then I would be okay with it. But only if Harrison wants to meet him."

"Fair enough." I add.

"Okay, last question. This one isn't as invasive," she says with a small smile. "What made you buy your house?"

I've been expecting this question. I shift a little in my seat, a bit nervous about how to answer. I had to really bargain with the guy who used to own the land. In the end, I offered him three times his asking price because I just had to have it. But I'm almost embarrassed to admit why—I don't want her to think I'm some kind of creep holding onto the past, but the place has always meant so much to me.

"Well, a few years ago, I ran into some money, and my dad helped me come up with a design for my dream house. I wanted it to be on the lake and close to Camp Willowbrooke. I figured there wasn't a better spot for me to buy other than our old fishing hangout."

"I knew it!" she exclaims, her cheeks turning a soft shade of pink. I can tell she's thinking of the same night we shared there. "So, you designed the house?" she asks.

"I did," I reply, taking a sip of my almost empty drink.

"It's beautiful from the outside," she says quietly, almost shy. "I'm a little embarrassed to admit this, but I've admired the house every day from my kitchen window. Even before I knew you lived there."

I can't help but smile. "I'm glad you like it. Maybe one day, when you're ready, you can take a look at the inside too."

24
Coraline

Dinner last night went a lot smoother than I anticipated. I really didn't know what to expect, but I'm just glad we were able to talk.

It actually sort of felt good, just like old times. He was my best friend for pretty much my entire adolescence. I'd be lying to myself if I said I didn't miss him and the friendship we shared.

It all still feels surreal. I almost feel like I'm living in some weird fantasy. The way he was looking at me at dinner last night was almost too much, but I also secretly loved it.

I plan on talking to Harrison this evening after I finish up at work. I have no idea how he is going to take the news, but I'll be so relieved to get it off of my chest.

Gemma is going to come over to play with Michael while I talk to Harrison in private. It's been really hard and confusing for Michael's little, four year old brain to comprehend that his daddy isn't coming back home. I don't want to confuse him even more by including him in the conversation tonight, especially if it goes badly.

I walk around the nurses station and pick up my next patient's chart, Edith Clearwater. I start flipping through the pages to see why she's here today and relax a little when I realize she's just here for a follow up from her cardiac event last week.

Her testimony that she gave in church has really stuck with me. It warmed my heart to hear the impact that God allows me to have on my patients' lives. Most people who work in healthcare get so numb to the traumatic situations that they go through. It's easy to forget that our bad days at work are sometimes the scariest day of someone's life.

How the patient is treated during those events is something that they'll never forget. This is something I find myself guilty of from time to time, especially when I worked in the inpatient hospital setting.

"Good evening Mrs.Clearwater. It's Coraline, may I come in?" I lightly knock on the door.

"Of course dear."

I walk inside of the room and take a seat on the stool. Edith is sitting on the examination table with her husband at her side.

Dr. Dawson, and his man purse full of drinks, took care of Edith while she was in the inpatient setting. I will be handling the follow up care from here on out unless something else happens.

"I read Dr. Dawson's notes from your hospital visit. How is everything going? Do you have any concerns that I can help you with?"

"Everything is going just fine. I haven't had any more symptoms and I've been taking it easy. I think I'm ready to start back in the garden again."

"I think that's a great idea." I agree while I complete my physical assessment. I listen to her heart and lungs with my stethoscope and review her vital signs. "Everything looks great."

"I just want to say thank you again, Coraline," she says, taking my hand in hers. "You're wonderful at what you do, and from what I've heard and seen, you're a great mama. Keep up the good work."

"Thank you, Mrs. Clearwater. I really appreciate that," I reply, my heart swelling a little at the kindness in her words.

"May I give you some advice?" she asks gently. I nod my head in response.

"One of the most important things I've learned in my life," she continues, her eyes steady, "is to put God first in everything that I do. Even when

I don't understand why I'm going through something or how I'm going to get through it, I just trust in Him. Don't ever forget to do that."

I made Harrison's favorite dinner tonight—homemade pizza casserole. I also baked some fresh cookies that smell absolutely delightful, much better than the burnt ones that Gemma tried to make a few weeks ago.

We sit down at the table together. I pick the seat with the best view of the lake house—Jesse's house. I still can't believe he owns it. If I could close my eyes and dream of the perfect house, it would be that one.

We eat in silence for a few minutes. I want to bring up the conversation, but each time I gather the courage, my anxiety takes over, and I lose it. I go through this cycle a few times before, finally, I find the strength to just get it over with.

"Harrison, sweetheart," I begin, my voice soft, "do you remember asking me about a photograph in my bedroom that you found?"

"Yes, the one of you and the oven dude."

"Yes, that one," I say, a small smile tugging at my lips. "The oven dude's name is Jesse Cooper. He used to be my best friend, and we loved each other very much."

"So what happened?" He asks, his brows furrowing in confusion.

"Mommy left town for college and moved to the city where you grew up," I begin, my voice steady. "It was there that I found out you were growing in my tummy."

Harrison looks up at me, still unsure, his eyes wide.

"I tried to tell your real father, but he never answered me. I just recently found out that he didn't even know about you and never got my messages.

Jesse Cooper—the oven dude, as you call him—he's your dad, Harrison."
I say while holding his gaze.

"Oh," Harrison says, taking another bite of his food.

"He truly didn't know you were born," I continue, my voice gentle. "I thought he did. But he knows now, and he'd like to get to know you. But only if you're comfortable with that."

"I guess that would be good. Will you be there too?" He looks up at me, uncertainty in his eyes.

"I will be if you want me to be, baby," I say, reaching across the table to squeeze his hand.

"What's he like, Mom?"

"He's funny, smart, and he has a dog," I reply, my heart swelling just a little. "I think if you give him a chance, he'll be a great dad."

"A dog! That's so cool! I wonder if he'll let me pet it," he grins, clearly excited by the idea.

He pauses for a minute and we eat in silence again.

"Hey, Mom... what if he gets to know me and doesn't like me?" His voice quiet and unsure.

"Oh bub, that's not possible. He's very excited to get to know the real you this time. There's not a doubt in my mind that he doesn't already love you."

25
Jesse

I'M SITTING AT THE head of the table in the conference room at Camp Willowbrooke for the celebration's final meeting. My stress has been through the roof, especially with everything going on in my personal life. I've been trying to maintain it in a healthy way but it's really getting to me today.

We had the Scottsdale Diner cater lunch for all the staff members attending the meeting. I wanted everyone to have something to enjoy while we go over the finishing touches. I even made a special request for Pamela's desserts.

I'm confident that we have as much in place as possible for this party to run smoothly. I anticipate a few hiccups and bumps in the road and have tried to plan accordingly. Hopefully nothing too crazy happens that we can't handle.

We have an emergency response team that has volunteered to hang out at the party and a security team as well. Dr. Dawson, the town's doctor, promised that he would stay on scene too.

I'm halfway through announcing my checklist when my phone beeps. I ignore it since I'm almost finished reviewing my plan with the team. My heart starts to race when I realize that it could be Coraline. I've been waiting for her response and it's been a few days since we met up.

I rush through the rest of the presentation and excuse myself from the room.

I pull out my phone and notice that I actually have two messages. One is from Cora, the other is from my dad. I choose to read Cora's message first.

> Hey Jess. I talked to Harrison last night and he has agreed to meet you. He requested that you come to our house and that you bring your dog. What day works best for you?

I can't stop the smile that spreads across my face. This is such great news.

> I'm free this rest of the week. Just let me know what day and the time. Lucy and I will be there. That's her name.

I was so nervous that he wouldn't want anything to do with me. I'm thankful that he's giving me a shot at fatherhood and that Cora had a change of heart.

I'd be lying if I said that a part of me isn't looking forward to hanging out with her too. I don't expect us to get back together, but man wouldn't that be something. It would be a testimony to how God's timing works and not our timing.

I pull up the messages from my dad next to see what he needed.

> Hey son, just checking in. I wanted to let you know that I talked to your mom the other day. She's okay, but she's taking some time off to let us calm down and have time to process everything.

> I also wanted to apologize again. I promise you that I had no idea that she was hiding this from us.

I've been trying my best not to think about my mother. I do feel bad for my dad, he doesn't deserve any of this. I send him a quick reply saying that I'll call him later and we will talk about everything. I think he will be excited to have a chance at being a grandfather.

I'm standing in my bedroom the next evening, staring at my reflection. Cora mentioned today would be a good day to get together, and I've been pacing around trying to figure out what to wear. I want to impress her—but not come off like I'm trying too hard.

After going back-and-forth with a few outfits, I settle on my new fishing t-shirt, my "good" jeans, and a clean pair of tennis shoes.

I throw on a hat and give myself a couple spritzes of cologne. It's the same scent I've worn for years—the one Cora always used to love.

"Are you ready Lucy girl?" I ask as I bend down to pat her head. She looks up at me, lets out a deep sigh and does a big stretch.

"I guess that means yes."

I make my way downstairs to the foyer. Tucked under my arm are two gift cards for the boys to the local toy store. I wasn't sure what they already had, so I figured it was safer to let them choose. This time, I made sure to check with Cora before buying anything. I'm doing my best to stay on her good side.

On the way out, I grab the bouquet from the table by the door. I ordered it from the local florist late last night—she owed me a favor, so she got it done fast. The flowers look good. I just hope Cora doesn't think I'm trying too hard. Even though I kind of am.

I grab my keys and load Lucy into the truck. She hops right into the front seat like she owns the place, tail thumping, tongue already hanging out.

I roll her window down before backing out of the driveway. Normally I don't keep her on a leash, but I want the boys to feel comfortable around her—so I clipped on her pink harness just in case.

We could've walked but it's been a while since we took a ride, and car rides are her absolute favorite. She leans into the breeze with her ears flapping and her tongue lolling out the side of her mouth—like the pig from that one old tv commercial. It makes me laugh, which I need.

As I turn into Cora's driveway, my stomach knots up tight. I can't stop thinking about Harrison and how all this must feel for him. I take a deep breath and remind myself: I won't let him down. Not on purpose. Not ever.

"God," I say softly, bowing my head and taking off my hat, "I want to start by thanking you for all the blessings you've given me. Thank you for bringing Cora back into my life and for her boys. I pray that Harrison will accept me as a father figure. Help me to be the best dad that I can be... to be someone he can look up to, like I look up to you."

I glance toward the front door, nerves still rattling under the surface.

"Lord, I just ask that this play date goes smoothly. That your will be done—whatever that looks like. I ask all of this in Jesus' name. Amen."

I turn the truck off and exit the vehicle. I grab Lucy's leash, the bouquet of flowers and the gift cards. I walk up the front porch and take a deep breath. I smile nervously at Lucy and go to knock on the door. As soon as I lift my fist, the door swings open.

"Jesse, it's so good to see you, please come in," Coraline says with her eyes bright.

The breath is stolen from my lungs. She's stunning and she doesn't even have to try. No makeup on, comfy clothes, and her hair a mess. God, I love it when she looks like this. Just real. Just Cora.

How did I ever let her get away from me? If I ever get another chance with her, there's no way I will ruin it.

26
Coraline

I HAVE TO REMIND myself to breathe and act like a normal human being tonight. My stomach has been in knots just thinking about all that could go wrong.

I haven't heard anything from Nash lately so that's a plus. I think. He must be behaving for now.

I'm starting to think that he triggered my PTSD when he left me all of those voicemails the other day. I've been way more anxious and on edge ever since. I started having nightmares again too.

Jesse showed up about an hour ago and not only did he bring Harrison and Michael each a small gift, he brought me flowers too—peach-toned daisies, soft pink roses, and tiny white flowers are woven throughout the arrangement.

I don't think he realizes how much it means to me. My stupid heart needs to calm down. Maybe he's just trying to set a good example for the kids? I need to stop reading into it.

Jesse's been playing a racing game on the TV with Harrison and Michael for a while now.

Harrison, surprisingly, hasn't stopped talking—he's been chatting Jesse's ear off the whole time they've been playing. Normally, he just glares at anyone who so much as looks in his direction, so this? This is excellent progress.

My heart feels a little lighter just watching them.

Lucy is laying beside Jesse and the kids on the floor. She let both of the boys waller her and attempt to rile her up. She's been an excellent dog this evening but, I have a feeling she always is.

I've tried my best not to hover but it's hard not to. I've genuinely enjoyed being a fly on the wall and just being able to observe them interact. It helps ease my anxiety.

Jesse's made a point to include Michael just as much as he includes Harrison, something that Nash never did. It warms my heart to see both of my kids having so much fun. I could easily get used to this and that's the part that scares me.

Harrison lets out a loud, joyful laugh when he beats Jesse in the race. Jesse throws his head back, laughing right along with him, and I don't even try to hide the butterflies fluttering in my stomach.

I've missed that sound—Harrison's real laugh. I didn't realize how much until it was gone. God, I just hope Jesse stays true to his word. I hope he sticks around, for the kids of course.

His eyes meet mine from across the room and soften. My mouth curves up into a smile. I swear it's like the entire room is charged with energy between us.

We hold each other's gaze for a long moment, until the tension feels too tight in my chest. I look away first and start to fidget with my hands to distract myself.

The playdate is over, and I'm walking Jesse and Lucy out to the truck.

"I feel like that went fantastic!" I exclaim. "I haven't seen both of my kids that excited or happy about something in a long time."

"I think it went well too." Jesse looks down at his feet, kicking a few pebbles as he speaks.

"Thanks again for the flowers, Jess," I say, giving his shoulder a brief, friendly squeeze. His blue eyes catch mine, and my stomach flutters in that familiar, electric way.

I pull my hand back, needing to put a little space between us.

"You don't have to thank me, Cora." His voice is light, with a smug grin creeping onto his face. "I'm just glad I could buy a pretty girl something that makes her smile."

He reaches up and tucks a strand of hair behind my ear, his fingers brushing against my skin. I feel my cheeks heat, and I bite my bottom lip to steady myself. My heart races, thudding in my chest like it's trying to break free.

His face is so close now, and he smells incredible. When did we get this close?

My mind starts spinning a thousand miles a minute, I'm terrified. If I let something rekindle between us, not only will he break my heart—but he could break theirs too.

I push the thoughts away, forcing myself to focus. I know I'm overthinking it, but I can't help it.

He stares at my lips and then he looks back up at my eyes. I swear he's leaning in, or did I imagine it? Nope, he's definitely leaning in.

"Lucy!" Michael yells as he bursts out of the house.

I jump back a couple of steps, and so does Jesse. It feels like we're two preteens caught by their parents, even though nothing happened. Just an awkward interruption by my son.

Michael is half-dressed—one shoe on, one shoe off, and already down to his boxers. "I forgot to give you a goodbye hug!" he says, wrapping Lucy in a vice grip. The poor dog just sits there, letting him shower her with affection.

"Alright, Michael," I say, walking over to him. "Leave the poor girl alone. Let's get inside and get ready for bed."

27
Jesse

IT'S EARLY SATURDAY MORNING, and I'm sitting on the front porch swing with Lucy and my old man. The weather's a perfect seventy degrees, and the sun's just beginning to rise. Birds are singing their songs, and everything feels still, like the world's waking up too.

It's the perfect kind of summer morning to enjoy a cup of coffee.

It's officially been a week since my first playdate with the kids. We've gotten together every evening since then, and things have been going better than I ever expected.

Harrison is still way better at his video games than I am, but I've learned something new too—Michael likes to bake.

The other night, we made a cake from scratch. Nothing caught on fire, and nothing broke. I'm calling that a win, considering I've never baked a thing in my entire adult life.

I also learned that the kids love riding bikes. Yesterday, the four of us rode them around Camp Willowbrooke. Cora and I used to ride bikes together every summer at the campground— it almost felt like old times. It's only better now because Harrison and Michael are here with us.

Cora has tagged along for every play date. The first time I came over, she didn't interact much and she mostly kept to herself. But now? Now she's right in the middle of the chaos. I've laughed more in the past few days than I have in over a year.

Being with all three of them has brought so much joy into my life. I didn't realize how much my heart could feel, how many emotions I could carry, until they came around.

"How are you feeling?" I ask my dad, breaking the quiet.

"Nervous. Excited. Happy. Too many things all at once," he replies, his gaze drifting toward the lake. His hands are folded neatly in his lap, but I can see the tension in his posture.

"I really think that you're going to fit right in with them. They're so smart and fun to be around. I bet they'll both have you wrapped around their little fingers before the day is over." I finish taking a sip of my drink and I notice that Cora and the kids are walking over from their house. She looks up at me and my dad and waves to us both.

The kids have never been on a boat and have never been fishing, so I decided today was the day. We're heading out on my boat, and it's going to be a learning experience for all of us. Plus, it'll be their first time meeting Papaw Lloyd—my dad.

The boys are decked out in matching rain boots and bucket hats, muscle t-shirts, and basketball shorts. Cora's in a loose-fitting t-shirt, jean shorts, sneakers, and a ball cap. Honestly, she could be wearing a trash bag, and I'd still think she looked stunning.

Harrison approaches the porch slowly, clearly skeptical of the new stranger. Michael, on the other hand, runs right past us, heading straight for Lucy without a second thought. He's always been like that—no hesitation, no fear.

I watch as he drops to his belly, getting right in Lucy's face. She greets him with a big, sloppy kiss on the cheek. Michael giggles.

"Hey guys," I say with a smile. "I want you all to meet someone. This is my dad, but you all can call him Papaw Lloyd. He's going to go fishing with us today, if that's alright with you two."

Neither of them say anything. I think they're too overstimulated and it's still too early in the morning for their little brains.

"Hi there, boys," Dad says, rising from his chair. He's wearing his bib overalls, an old hat, and fishing boots—the uniform of someone who's spent years on the water. "It's a pleasure to meet you both."

"Hi!" Michael says, his voice full of enthusiasm, barely looking up as he continues to waller all over Lucy.

Harrison is the more skittish one and he offers dad a small smile and wave. At least he didn't glare at him like he does everyone else. I warned my dad that Harrison would probably be shy and reserved until he got comfortable.

Papaw Lloyd gets down on one knee so he can be eye level with the kids. "Do you all mind if I tag along today? I'd really like to get to know you two better."

"I guess so," Harrison says as he shrugs his shoulders.

"I'm so excited to get on the boat!" Michael zooms around the porch like a wild animal. He is full of energy this morning. I wish I could have a fraction of his energy for a day.

Harrison joins Michael on the porch and pets Lucy. "Hey girl, I missed you so much." He gives her a huge hug and she looks up at him with a loving gaze.

He then turns his attention back to me with an ornery expression on his face. "Oven dude, I really love your dog."

I burst out laughing and shake my head. "Oven dude? I thought we were past that. I thought we were friends now?"

"Oh yeah, you're right." He giggles and gives me a hug. He's so rotten.

I clap my hands together and stand up. "Okay everyone, time to head out to the dock. Boys, I got you both your own rods and tackle boxes. Cora, I got you a pink one for you." I wink and she rolls her eyes. I don't miss the smile that she tries to hide.

"Lets go!" Michael takes off in the direction of the dock.

"Slow down, Michael!" Cora calls out as she starts jogging to catch up with him. "Be careful! Don't get too close to the water until we're all down there together!"

Meanwhile, Harrison, Dad, and I make our way down to the wooden boat dock in a comfortable silence. Dad's holding all the fishing poles, Harrison's got the lunch sacks, and I'm carrying the tackle boxes. It's a small, simple moment, but it feels like we've done this a thousand times before.

Harrison gasps when the dock comes into view. My boat—a big, early 2000's fish and ski model—sits there, looking as solid as ever. It's big enough to fit six adults comfortably. When I first bought it, I'd just sold my software, and I didn't want to draw too much attention to myself by spending a fortune on something brand new. But I really wanted one, so I settled on this one.

"What do you all think? Isn't she a beaut?" I ask, slipping into my best *Christmas Vacation* impression, a sly grin tugging at my lips.

"This is the coolest thing ever, bro!" Harrison yells, jumping up and down, clearly over the moon.

"Shhh!" Cora says, her hands up in an attempt to calm them down. "You're going to scare the fish away before we even get started."

Once everyone's on the boat and all of our supplies are secured, I back us out of the dock.

There's still a coat of mist hovering over the water this early in the morning. Instead of looking eerie, I feel like it's kind of cozy. This is the best time to be out on the water, right before the summer heat scorches us.

The scent of the lake, fish, and gas from the boat soothes my soul. I love being out here, on the water. I silently pray this is just the first of many fishing trips for us as a family.

Once we pass the buoys, I give the boat a little more gas, speeding up. Out of the corner of my eye, I catch sight of Cora, and I can't help but chuckle. She has a death grip on both of the kids, holding them like they're about to launch into space.

"Are you boys excited to fish today?" I ask, glancing back at them.

"I am! I'm going to catch all the fishes that live in the waters!" Michael says in a rush, his voice full of enthusiasm.

"My goal is to catch one and to be able to eat it later," Harrison states, sounding proud of his more practical approach.

"I bet we can make that happen," Papaw Lloyd chimes in with a grin. "Your dad makes the best fish fry around town." The excitement on his face is contagious, and for a second, I see a spark in his eyes I haven't seen since the days when I played high school football.

After a few minutes of driving the boat around, I pull up to one of my favorite fishing spots. I grab my bait container and get the poles lined up. My dad is going to be in charge of the trolling motor so we will be coasting a little bit.

"Alright, who wants to go first?" I ask, glancing at the kids.

"Me!" Michael yells, practically jumping out of his seat with his hands in the air. Cora shoots him a "shh" that's as gentle as she can, trying not to hurt his feelings.

"Excuse me, sorry," he whispers, his excitement bubbling over. "I'm just excited."

"It's okay, bud. Come here." I motion for him to walk over, and when he does, I hand him his fishing pole. Reaching into my bait container, I pull out a fat, wriggling nightcrawler worm, its body squirming in my hands.

"Do you want to help me put the worm on the hook?" I hold the worm out to him and he jumps back and as far away from me as he can.

"EW!" He makes a disgusted face. "No way!"

"I'll do it," Harrison says, getting out of his seat and taking the rod from his brother.

"Okay then," I reply. "I'll hold the hook and walk you through how to wrap the worm on it so it won't fall off when you cast."

Harrison takes the nightcrawler from me, his expression never changing as he expertly threads the worm onto the hook like he's done it a hundred times before.

"Are you sure you've never done this?" I ask with a smile, impressed by how quickly he caught on.

"I've always wanted to, but this really is my first time," Harrison says, his voice steady but with a hint of excitement.

"Well, you're going to be a pro in no time." I wink at him, giving him a playful nudge.

I move him into position to cast the line, making sure to explain every step carefully. I emphasize, "Make sure to aim out, and don't forget—no swinging the pole around or letting the hook get too close to anyone."

As I talk, I can't help but notice the slight anxiety on Cora's face. I'm sure as a nurse, she's seen her fair share of fishing injuries. She's probably imagining the worst-case scenario.

"Here goes nothing," Harrison says, holding up his fishing pole with determination. He casts it exactly how I showed him, and to my surprise, he nails it on his first try. He's a natural. I guide him through reeling the line back in, and he does it with the ease of someone who's been doing this for years.

"He didn't get anything," Michael says, his brow furrowing in confusion. "Why didn't he catch anything?"

"You see, Michael," my dad begins, his voice calm and steady, "fishing is a test of something called patience. It's not about how many fish you catch or even if you catch any at all. Fishing is about learning to wait, to listen, and most of all, to have patience."

Michael looks up at him, completely serious, and deadpans, "But I don't want to wait. I just want to win. I want to catch the most fish."

"Although they do have something called a fishing tournament, this isn't one," my dad continues, his tone lighthearted. "This boating trip is all about learning, not winning."

Just then, Harrison's line jerks. "What was that? What do I do?" he asks, eyes wide.

"You've got a bite, baby!" Cora exclaims, her voice full of excitement. "Reel it in!"

"Wait, don't reel it in yet!" I call out. "You've got to set the hook first, just like we talked about."

Harrisons battle with the fish was short but thrilling. The fish that came out of the water was about six or seven inches, so a pretty excellent catch for his first time. The fish that he caught ended up being a crappie, one of my favorite fish to eat.

I show Harrison how to carefully remove the fish from the hook and place it in the boat's compartment, designed to store the catch. "Great job, Harrison! I'm so proud of you!"

Harrison smiles up at me, then wraps his arms around me, resting his head on my chest. "Thanks, Jesse."

As I look over his shoulder, I catch Cora's eye. She's looking at me with the biggest smile on her face and for a moment, everything feels right.

28
Jesse

FISHING WENT BETTER THAN I expected. I'd been nervous about the kids getting bored, but they both really got into it. The overcast weather turned out to be perfect for fishing. No one got too hot and we all had a great time.

By the end of the day, both of the kids had really warmed up to my dad. I even noticed him wipe away a tear or two when we were all together.

Harrison ended up catching two crappie, Michael caught two bluegill, my dad landed a bass, and Cora... well, Cora accidentally caught a turtle. As for me? I caught nothing.

Honestly, I wasn't even mad. I had an incredible time teaching my sons how to fish and spending the day with my new little family.

We're currently back at my house and I'm frying the fish that we caught for dinner. Harrison and my dad filleted and prepped the fish together so we could eat them. Michael thought it was gross and wanted nothing to do with it.

While we were busy getting the fish ready to fry, Harrison casually mentioned something he'd learned during the latest church service.

"We talked about the story where Jesus fed over five thousand people with just two fish and five loaves of bread," he said. "A little boy gave Jesus his lunch and then, bam, it turned into enough food for everyone."

That moment really struck me. It was the perfect opportunity to witness to him. As I shared my thoughts with him, I was reminded that children really do listen, sometimes more than we realize, especially when we think they're not paying attention.

Cora sits down across from me, Michael at her side. Harrison is nestled between me and my dad. We all join hands and say a prayer to bless the food and thank God for providing it.

"This is really cool, Dad," Harrison says after swallowing his first bite.

My heart skips a beat. He called me *dad*. This is all I've ever wanted, and it's finally happening.

When I first found out about Harrison, I was angry at myself for missing so much of his life. But now, sitting here, I know that God's timing is never wrong.

"I'm glad you think so," I reply and smile. I look at Cora and I see her quickly wipe a tear from her face.

"Papaw Lloyd?" Harrison looks at my dad, "Thank you for teaching me how to get the fish ready. I had a good time today."

"Me too! This was the bestest day ever!" Michael says in between bites of food.

"I'm truly honored that I was allowed to tag along with you all," my dad says, his voice sincere. "Thank you again, Coraline. You don't know how much this has meant to me."

We continue to eat in comfortable silence, the weight of the day settling in, until it's time to clean up. Cora wipes her mouth with a napkin, then clears her throat. "Do you boys want to go in the living room and watch TV with Lucy? Jesse and I will take care of the dishes and clean up."

"Coraline," my dad says, folding his hands together nervously. "If it would be okay, I'd very much like to play a game with them."

"That sounds wonderful," Cora replies with a smile. "We hooked their game system up to the main TV just a little bit ago, so it should be ready."

The boys took off enthusiastically, with my dad in tow, while Cora stood up to start collecting the silverware. She was in the middle of picking up a glass plate when it slipped from her hand, shattering into tiny pieces on the floor.

"Shoot," she whispered under her breath, her brow furrowing in frustration. She bent down to start picking up the broken glass, but then winced. She pulled her hand back quickly, grabbing at her finger.

"Are you okay?" I asked, immediately stepping toward her.

"Yeah, I'm fine. I think it's just a scratch," she muttered, but I could see the pain in her eyes.

"Let me go grab my first aid kit and I'll take a look at it." I stand up and turn on my heel before she can protest.

When I walk back into the dining room, Cora's sitting down in a chair holding a wet paper towel around her finger.

"Here, let me see it." She winces again as I grab her hand.

I get down on one knee and inspect the cut. It's a mild cut from the glass, more than just a scratch, but at least there's no glass embedded in her skin—that's a relief. I open up the first aid kit and gather the supplies I need.

Gently, I take a q-tip and apply some antibiotic ointment, followed by a fresh band-aid.

She sits in silence, her honey-colored eyes studying me as I work, her gaze soft and unwavering.

"Thank you, Jess," she whispers, just loud enough for me to hear. "You didn't have to do that."

"It's my pleasure," I reply honestly. "You shouldn't have to take care of everything by yourself. You do so much for everyone. I know it's nice to have someone look after you for a change."

I reach up and tuck a strand of hair behind her ear, my fingers brushing against her skin. I notice the way her breath hitches slightly at the touch, and for a moment, I want to close the distance between us, kiss her, and see where things go.

Before I can make up my mind, she turns away, picking up around the table as if nothing happened. We fall into a familiar rhythm, clearing the table together and loading the dishwasher. The sound of the dishes clinking fills the space, but there's an undercurrent of something much more tender between us.

I'd be lying if I said she didn't look perfect in my home. The sight of her here, with the kids, feels right—like this is where we're meant to be.

I could get used to this. I hope and pray that one day, it will become my reality.

"This week has been great, with you and the kids," she says, wiping her hands on a towel, her voice soft but steady.

"It really has," I agree, my voice quieter than usual.

She takes a step closer to me, just close enough that I can feel the heat radiating off of her. The air between us feels thick with tension, and I swear I can almost *feel* the attraction that's been building all week.

I look up at her again, and before I can stop myself, I lean a little closer. Her lips are right there, so close that I can almost taste the words that are hanging between us. I want to kiss her more than anything right now.

"I've enjoyed spending time with you again, Cora," I murmur, my breath mingling with hers as our noses brush.

Her lips brush mine once and she pulls back, as if she starts to regret her decision. "I'm sorry, are you—" I don't give her time to finish her sentence. I take the opportunity. I grab her face, my hands desperate to hold her, and I kiss her fiercely. It's a kiss full of hunger and need, of all the years that I've spent missing her. She leans into me and opens her mouth to kiss me back. A soft groan escapes me.

I thread my fingers into her hair, holding her close. She grabs onto me, pulling me even closer, and for the first time in years, everything feels right. It's just me and her.

When we finally pull apart, my heart is racing, and it takes a full minute for me to catch my breath. I open my eyes slowly, still feeling the thrum of that kiss and the rush of emotions that came with it.

That was worth the wait.

29
Coraline

It's Sunday morning, the boys are awake and are excited to go back to church today. Jesse will be there and I haven't been able to stop thinking about him since the kiss we shared. It was perfect.

Harrison is dressed and sitting at the table, happily eating a cherry pastry. His messy curls are tamed down this morning.

Michael is licking the icing off of his pastry without actually eating it, which is no surprise. The kid loves sugar and icing. His hair is spiked up into a little mohawk.

"Mom," Harrison starts, "I have a question."

"What is it, sweetheart?" I ask, pouring my coffee into my favorite cup. The kitchen is filled with the familiar, rich, comforting smell of fresh coffee.

I glance out the window and see that Lucy, Jesse's dog, is sprawled across his front porch, soaking up the morning sun like she owns it.

"Do you think you'll ever get back together with my dad?" Harrison asks.

"Only time will tell," I say, giving a small shrug. "Would you two like it if we started seeing each other again? You know... as boyfriend and girlfriend?"

"Yes!" they both exclaim in unison, their faces lighting up.

"I have a question too, Mommy," Michael chimes in, his voice full of seriousness.

I nod my head and lift my eyebrows in encouragement.

"What about my daddy? Will you ever get back with him?" he says with a small frown. "I do like our new daddy, but I miss seeing my old one."

My heart shatters all over again. I expected him to start asking about Nash, but it's so hard to explain to a four year old that their dad is in jail.

"No, baby," I say, looking into Michael's big brown eyes. "Mommy won't be getting back together with him. I know you miss him, and I know you love him, and that's okay. But he did some bad things, and he won't be coming back. I know that's hard for you to understand, and I'm so sorry. Maybe one day, when you're a little older, you can go and see him."

Michael nods slowly, his small face full of quiet understanding.

"That's okay," he says softly. "I like Jesse. He's so much nicer than my other daddy. He never raises his voice or gets mad at me or nothing."

My heart sinks and rises at the same time. I didn't even know that was possible. It sinks because of how terrible Nash was to us. It rises because of how good of an influence Jesse is to them. But it rises because of how steady and kind Jesse is to them. How he's become a quiet but constant source of calm in their lives.

We arrive at Grace Haven right on time and scurry into the pew that we've made our own these past few weeks with Shae. She raises an accusatory eyebrow when she sees me. I haven't told her about the kiss yet. She knows that Jesse has been spending time with the kids but nothing more than that.

I glance to my left and see him sitting a few rows over. Our eyes meet almost instantly, and my stomach does a little flip. I can't help but blush, the warmth creeping up my neck as I offer him a small, nervous smile.

Instead of smiling back, Jesse stands up and walks toward me. My heart jumps, beating wildly in my chest. Each step he takes feels like it's in slow motion, and for a brief moment, I wonder if I'm even breathing.

He's been putting the kids and me first ever since he found out about Harrison. I'm thankful that God helped me to let go of all the anger that I had been so desperate to hold on to. It feels so good to not bear that burden anymore.

"Good morning, Cora. Hello, boys," Jesse says, his voice calm and warm as he gives each of them a fist bump. His eyes linger on me for just a second before he looks down at them. "Do you all mind if I sit here?"

"Of course not," I reply quickly, the words coming out before I even think about it. My heart is still racing, but I keep my voice steady. We all scoot down to make room for him.

My anxiety decides to activate at that moment and I suddenly become self conscious. The entire congregation can see us all sitting together. It's not exactly a secret that we were high school sweethearts. I know some of the older folks are probably whispering about it.

I'm hyper-aware of everything around me. My hands feel too sweaty and my breathing feels too fast, too loud. Oh my gosh I hope I don't smell bad too. I might have horrible coffee breath right now.

Throughout the entire church service, I swear I can feel his presence beside me—like it's tangible, like he's a part of me in a way that I haven't felt in so long.

Every time I sneak a glance at him out of the corner of my eye, I almost have the urge to pinch myself. Is this real? Am I really sitting here, beside him, in front of everyone?

And then I notice it—his leg is shaking, too. He's nervous, just like I am. It's strangely comforting, knowing I'm not the only one with butterflies fluttering around inside.

Despite the nerves, we're sitting together, the four of us, as a family. At this point I know Shae knows something has happened. She keeps smirking at me and giving me a knowing look.

"I'll explain later," I silently mouth to her.

I'm all too aware of his open hand resting beside me, just inches from mine. I know that move—it's one of the oldest tricks in the book to get someone to hold your hand.

I don't think. I just reach down, my hand trembling slightly as I slide it into his. We both hold still for a moment. He looks down at our entwined hands and then back up at me, his gaze steady. We hold eye contact for just a second too long. Just enough time to make it clear that we're not *just* friends anymore.

I don't look away. Instead, I embrace the moment, feeling a quiet, sure confidence rise in me. I've decided that I'm okay with this. I'm okay with taking this step forward together. Because, at this point in life, if we don't take the chances God gives us, if we keep holding back, we'll always be left with that "what if?" hanging over us.

And I don't want any more "what ifs" with Jesse. Not anymore. I want to take this chance—whatever it leads to—even if it means risking my heart again.

After Pappy finishes his sermon, he nods to my Granna, who's already making her way up to the piano to play for the altar call. He does this every service—offers the chance for someone to come forward and be saved at the old-fashioned altar of prayer. It's something I've seen countless times growing up, but today, it feels different.

As a teenager, I'd responded to an altar call one Wednesday night and dedicated my life to God. Since then, I haven't really felt the pull to come forward again. Not in the way I do now.

I feel it deep in my chest, this quiet tug, a call I can't ignore.

I've made a lot of mistakes in the past few years. I'm not perfect, and I never will be. But I suppose that's why He calls us *as we are*—broken, flawed, and in need of grace.

I've backslid. I've strayed far from the path, away from God, away from the church. I've let my pride get in the way. I've been too afraid of what people might think, too consumed with shame about my sins to do what I knew I needed and wanted to do.

A few weeks ago, I felt this same pull to come forward, but I ignored it. I was too stubborn and caught up in my own doubts and fears.

But today... today, I don't care who's watching.

I'm done hiding. I'm done pretending like everything's fine when I know deep down that I need to make it right with God.

So, without thinking any more about it, I stand up, my legs shaky, but my heart sure. Jesse's hand tightens slightly in mine, as if to steady me, but he doesn't stop me. He knows.

The boys look up at me, and for a brief moment, I wonder if they understand the weight of this decision. But I don't give myself time to second guess.

I walk down the aisle, the familiar feeling of the altar pulling me in, calling me back to a place I once knew so well. It's humbling. It's terrifying. But it's also the most freeing thing I've done in years.

There, at the altar, with my family by my side, I give my heart fully back to Jesus. I repent of my sins, of the choices I made that led me here, and I rededicate my life to God.

The weight on my shoulders lifts just a little, replaced by the warmth of grace. I feel... whole again. Not perfect, but forgiven. And that, for now, is enough.

30
Coraline

I FEEL AN EXTRA pep in my step as I walk up the steps into the Scottsdale Clinic. I feel different. Stronger. More at peace with myself than I have in a long time.

Yesterday felt so freeing. After I went to the altar, the whole church sang *'Amazing Grace'*. There were lots of happy tears and hugs. I was so caught up that I didn't have time to talk to Shae because we had to leave and go straight to Granna and Pappy's.

I have my iced coffee in one hand and I use the other to open the door. I've gotten into a good routine these past few weeks of working here. I've established a great relationship with my patients and my new work family. For the first time in a while, I'm really *present* in my work, not distracted by the noise of everything going on in my life.

When I walk in, Shae is sitting at the front desk waiting for me. She's sipping her drink and looking at me with her eyebrows raised, waiting for me to fill her in.

"Okay, so I know you're on to me," I say, throwing my hands up in mock surrender.

"On to you? Coraline, the whole congregation and anyone with eyes can see the way you two have been looking at each other." She sits her drink down, the smirk widening as she folds her arms across her chest. "It's more than obvious that something's happened. I'm just glad that it finally did."

My mouth drops open in disbelief. I totally thought she was going to be against us seeing each other, that she'd have some kind of lecture ready for me. But here she is, giving me an unexpected stamp of approval.

"Is it *that* obvious?" I whisper, my face flushing. I cringe inwardly, but I can't help it—this whole thing feels so new, so raw.

"Yes," she deadpans. "Now are you going to tell me about it or what?"

I start off by briefing her about the play dates with the kids. I tell her about the fishing excursion with Lloyd yesterday and how happy the kids were. I mention the building tension over the past few days and the kiss. She squealed when I told her about it.

"I am so happy for you guys," Shae says as she pulls me into a hug, squeezing me tight. I can feel the genuine warmth in her embrace.

"Yeah," I reply as I hug her back, "I am too. That's enough about me, though. How are *you* doing?"

"I'm living the dream," Shae jokes, rolling her eyes with her signature sass.

"Aren't we all," I snort, making a face. "But really, are you and John still doing good? I haven't heard you talk about him much lately."

"We're doing okay," she says, her voice softening just a little. "I've just been stressed out over wedding planning, and he's been swamped with his job." She looks off into space for a moment, her expression distant, like she's trying to process something.

I know that look—it's the same one she gets when she's not fully ready to talk about whatever's weighing on her.

"Yeah, I heard about the cow incident," I say, trying to lighten the mood, knowing she'll appreciate a good laugh.

Shae exhales with a chuckle. "Yeah, that was something else. Day in the life of the town's only emergency vet," she adds, her tone dry but amused.

She stands up from her chair, stretching as she walks toward the filing cabinet, pulling out charts and organizing them with practiced ease. It's a slow day today, which is a relief.

I lean against the counter, watching her work. "Are you still planning on getting married next year?" I prod gently, trying to bring it back to her and John.

"I think so," she replies with a shrug, her voice a little uncertain, like she's still weighing the decision.

"You think so?" I ask, confused. "I feel like there's something you're not telling me."

Shae slams the file cabinet door a little harder than necessary, and I can see her frustration flicker in her eyes before she turns around to face me. "I'm half tempted to call it off and just go to the courthouse. It would definitely be less stressful, and cheaper."

The words hit me like a ton of bricks. I hadn't realized just how much she was carrying. "Well, that I can understand," I say softly, "but only if it's what *you both* want."

I start to feel a wave of guilt wash over me. I've been so caught up in my own life, in the whirlwind of the past few days, that I didn't even stop to check in on my best friend. Shae has always been there for me. She's always been the one to listen to me when I needed to vent, and here I am, barely noticing how much she's struggling.

"If there's any way I can help you, just let me know," I offer.

Her shoulders slump slightly, and she lets out a breath like she's been holding it in for a while. "I think I will take you up on that offer," she says, her voice a little softer than before.

"We can make it fun! I've never been married and I've only been to one wedding my whole life, but I will do whatever I can." It does kind of make me excited to be able to help her. I enjoy planning birthday parties for my kids and I'm fairly decent at it. "I'll start doing some research ASAP."

"Thanks Cora. I appreciate it."

"You don't have to thank me, Shae!" I say, my voice thick with emotion. "I just wish you would've said something sooner."

She sighs, looking down at the folders in her hands like she's trying to gather the strength to say something she's been holding back. "You've just had so much going on—moving, Nash, and now Jesse. I didn't think you needed my stress too."

She bites the inside of her cheek, trying to hold back whatever it is that's weighing on her, her eyes never quite meeting mine. "But it's okay. I have thick skin and big shoulders. I'll get through it. It'll be fine."

I feel a lump form in my throat. "I know it will, but I just want you to know that you shouldn't have to do it alone! And just in case there's something going on that you're not ready to talk about yet, I want to remind you that you can talk to me. I won't judge you, Shae. I want to be here for you, just like you're always here for me."

The words hit her, and I can see the struggle in her eyes as her gaze flickers between the floor and my face. Her eyes begin to swim with unshed tears, and I can tell she's fighting hard not to blink them away, to keep her composure.

I reach forward, taking the folders gently from her hands, and pull her into a hug.

"I love you, Shae. And I'm not going anywhere."

She whimpers softly against my shoulder, her body finally giving in to the tears she's been holding back. She nods her head, her arms wrapping around me tightly, and I feel the weight she's been carrying start to lift, even if just a little.

"Why don't you head home for the day?" I suggest. "We're not that busy. I think we can handle it."

"No, I can't do that to you all. I would feel awful." She takes a tissue from the front desk and blots at the mascara from under her eyes.

"Well, I feel awful that you're hurting and you have to pretend like everything's okay at work. Stop for some coffee and get a sweet treat on the way home. Maybe do some self care and try to relax?"

"What about Dr. Dawson?" Shae asks, still reluctant to give in.

"What about him?" I reply with a shrug. "He'll understand. You never take time off, and I guarantee you have more PTO than all of us combined. Go home! Take a mental health day. I've got this!"

I make a shoo motion with my hands, and after a second of hesitation, she finally gives in with a heavy sigh.

"Fine, fine. But if you need anything—"

"I'll call you, don't worry," I say, giving her a teasing grin. "Now go take care of yourself."

She grabs her purse and heads toward the door. I watch her go, still wishing she would let me in on whatever's really going on. But for now, I'll just have to be patient.

I pick up my iced coffee and finish it in one go, the cold sweetness hitting me with a jolt of energy. I'm definitely going to need more of this today.

But for Shae... I just hope that, whenever she's ready, she opens up to me. She hardly ever gets upset, and that's what worries me. Something is off, I can feel it, but she's not one to show vulnerability easily.

I say a quick prayer for her, hoping she finds the peace she needs, and just as I finish, the front door to the clinic opens with a soft chime, signaling our first patient of the day.

31
Coraline

It's the first night of the 100th year celebration for Camp Willow-brooke, and I can already feel the energy buzzing in the air. The clinic closed early tonight, not long after Shae went home. I was able to leave at the same time as Granna and Pappy, so I opted to follow behind them as they made their way to the campground.

There's a schedule posted, listing all the daily activities, but for now the campground isn't doing anything too big tonight.

Pappy hauls his fifth-wheel camper with the old truck he's had since before I was born. It's always been a point of pride for him, even though the truck's seen better days. The camper is the only thing he's actually upgraded over the years. I think my grandparents actually got a bigger camper in hopes that me and the kids would start going with them every year and now it's actually happening.

When we first turn down the camp entrance, I roll my windows down and take a deep breath, inhaling the smoky scent of campfire that drifts through the air. The corners of my mouth turn upward as I breathe it in. That smell, that familiar, earthy scent, brings back all kinds of memories.

I'm flooded with images of Gemma and I—our laughter ringing through the trees, playing in the creek, riding our bikes all over the camp-grounds, and spending hours on end at the park. We would play from the time the sun came up until we fell asleep, worn out, sitting on Pappy's lap around the campfire, listening to his stories.

I smile as I glance over at the boys, watching them in the rearview mirror. I'm so happy that my kids get to experience that too.

We eventually pull up to site fourteen, one of our old favorite spots. It's right beside of the park and I'll be able to sit in my camping chair while I watch the boys play.

The creek runs right behind the campsite. It's the perfect spot for little adventures, even if it rains. I remember Granna used to give Gemma and I each an umbrella and a pair of rain boots, and we would run around in the rain together, jumping in puddles.

I park my car, get the boys out and grab their bikes from the bike mount. I figured that they could play or ride their bikes while I help set up the campsite.

"Be careful boys! Watch out for the other campers!" I yell as the boys take off to the park together.

I can see and hear them from our campsite so I feel comfortable letting them go by themselves. There's already a few kids playing who look to be around their ages.

One of the girls that Harrison is playing with looks like Charlie's daughter, Jenny. They occasionally go to Grace Haven and I think she's in the same class as Harrison.

While the kids play, Granna and I help guide Pappy while he backs the camper into the actual campsite. Trying to park a camper is not an easy task, especially a fifth wheel. It's so unnecessarily stressful.

My Granna used to joke and say that real love was staying together after trying to park the camper because it's so frustrating. It's the only time my grandparents would bicker, and I'd laugh as they exchanged playful jabs, trying to guide the camper into place. But, by the time they finished leveling the camper and we sat down to eat supper, the tension was always gone. It was replaced with laughter and the comfort of being together.

I catch myself smiling as I watch Pappy working with his usual determination, getting everything just right. The little arguments between him and Granna always make me feel like home, reminding me that no matter how many years go by, some things never change.

After Pappy finishes with the leveling, Granna and I start pulling the awning down and getting the string lights ready to hang. The warm evening light starts to filter through the trees. I can already imagine how beautiful the campsite will look once it's all set up.

That's when I see Gemma pulling in with Goose, and a wave of excitement rushes through me. I haven't seen her in a while, and the sight of her familiar face instantly brings back memories of our childhood here.

"Gemma!" I call out, waving with both hands.

Her face lights up as she spots me, and she waves back. Goose is riding shotgun beside her. The moment she steps out of the car, I can feel the energy shift. It's the kind of joy that only family can bring.

Granna's eyes soften, and a smile tugs at her lips when she see's them. Even though Gemma's always been the free spirit of the family, you can see how much she means to Granna.

"Hey, guys! Where are the kiddos?" Gemma calls, her voice carrying in the crisp evening air as she hooks Goose up to his leash.

Goose, the golden retriever, prances out of the car like he owns the place. His golden fur is so shiny it almost looks like it's been professionally blow-dried before they left for the campground. I can't help but roll my eyes and smile.

He's one of the most pampered dogs I know, mainly because his mom is an esthetician and owns a salon. Gemma's all about self-care and pampering, and that extends to her beloved pup. She firmly believes that everyone—humans and animals alike—deserve a little TLC.

"Good grief," I mutter under my breath, laughing softly. "Goose looks better than I do right now."

Gemma smirks, unbothered. "Well, you know what they say... dogs are a reflection of their owner."

I shake my head with a grin, amused by how easily she manages to get away with treating her dog like a little celebrity.

"The kids are over at the park playing. I've been keeping an eye on them while we get everything situated," I reply, brushing my hands together as I walk over to Goose.

"Hello, handsome," I say in my best baby talk voice, bending down to pet him.

Goose's tail starts wagging furiously, and he eagerly sniffs my face. His cold nose boops my cheek, and I nearly lose my balance, stumbling a bit. Goose, oblivious to his size. I laugh at his gentle but clumsy enthusiasm.

"You big goof," I chuckle, scratching behind his ears. Goose looks up at me with those soulful eyes. He's about to leave a trail of dog hair all over my clothes, but it doesn't matter. He's the kind of dog you just can't stay mad at.

"I'm going to go say hi to them," Gemma says, standing up straight and brushing off her hands. She glances back at me. "I can stay over there with them if you want?"

"Yeah that sounds great! I think that we have it all handled here. We did most of the inside stuff yesterday." I wipe sweat off of my brow. "Are you staying tonight or just visiting?"

"I'm still thinking about it. We'll see," she says as she turns around and starts walking to the park with Goose at her side, trotting along.

I watch Gemma greet the boys and then I notice something that peaks my interest. I was correct when I thought I saw Jenny because Charlie is now sitting on the bench by the swing set. When he notices my sister, his entire body language changes. I make a mental note to ask her what that's all about later.

I turn back to our campsite, feeling a quiet sense of peace settle over me. The kids, the memories, and everything falling into place—it feels like everything I've been hoping for is finally coming together.

After everything's finished, Granna and I start working on dinner. We wanted something simple and easy so we picked spaghetti. The camper has a gas stove and an oven large enough to cook for all of us. Really the only thing that the kitchen in this camper doesn't have is a dishwasher.

"How does it feel to be camping again?" Granna asks, her voice soft and warm as she works on the noodles and garlic bread.

I pause for a moment, letting the scent of the campfire mix with the familiar smells of dinner. I take a deep breath, feeling the calm of the campground settle into my bones. "Honestly, really good. My soul loves being here. It's so peaceful, and I'm really excited for the kids."

I start chopping an onion, the sharp smell filling the air.

Granna looks up from her work, her hands moving slower as she glances over at me. "I'm so glad that you decided to come. I miss spending time with you and your sister so much that it hurts my heart sometimes," she admits, her voice quiet.

Her words hit me like a wave, and suddenly I'm fighting the lump in my throat. Only my grandmother would say something so raw and vulnerable that it pulls on my heartstrings and makes me want to cry—especially while I'm chopping an onion.

I force a smile, trying to keep my composure. "I miss it too, Granna. I miss how things used to be… before everything changed."

She nods, a sadness in her eyes that reflects mine. "I know, dear. Life has a way of throwing curveballs, doesn't it? But we make the most of what we have now."

I set the knife down for a moment, my hands resting on the counter.

Granna smiles softly, reaching over to squeeze my hand. "We've always got each other, no matter what."

I hear a loud thump outside and the camper door swings open.

"Boys! Do not go in there!" Gemma squeals, but it's too late. Goose jumps inside, mud splattering everywhere as Harrison and Michael giggle behind him, their faces alight with pure mischief.

Harrison and Michael both look like they've been taking turns rolling in the mud. I'm starting to think that's exactly what happened.

"What are you all doing?" I screech as they make their muddy entrance. "You can't come inside of the camper covered in mud!"

Before anyone can respond, Michael, full of energy and excitement, runs straight to Granna and gives her a big bear hug, sending mud everywhere. I gasp, but Granna just chuckles, her eyes twinkling with nostalgia.

"Oh, Coraline, it's okay," Granna says gently, patting Michael's back as he clings to her. "I would do anything for you and Gemma to be this little again and covered in mud from playing together."

I stare at Granna, wide-eyed, not sure how to react to the absolute mess my kids and Goose have just made. But the warmth in Granna's voice makes me pause, and I realize she's right. This is what childhood is about. The mess, the joy, and the memories they'll carry with them.

"Well, I suppose I can't be mad at them if they're having this much fun," I admit with a sigh, a small smile tugging at my lips despite the chaos.

Granna looks at me knowingly, a slight smile curving her lips. "No, you can't. Just let them be kids, dear."

The boys, grinning from ear to ear, continue to cause a ruckus inside the camper, with Goose happily shaking off the mud as he trots around the small space, oblivious to the mess he's creating.

"But your camper. They're getting mud everywhere!" Gemma is stuck with her hands over her mouth at the door. Goose is sitting on the pullout couch on top of all of our clean linen that we just put on yesterday.

"It makes for a great life lesson. Once they are all cleaned up, they will help mop up the floors and change the sheets again. Isn't that right boys?"

"Yes, Granna," Harrison says softly. "I'm sorry mommy. We were just excited and forgot how dirty we were."

"It's okay. I think I overreacted a little," I confess. "By the time you all are cleaned up and clean the camper, supper will be ready."

Harrison and Michael zoom ahead on their bikes, their laughter echoing through the campground. Gemma and I walk leisurely behind them, both of us keeping a watchful eye as the boys weave in and out of the dirt paths, racing each other.

Goose trots happily beside us, his tail swishing in time with his steps. He's been on his best behavior since the mud fiasco in the camper. Every now and then, he glances up at us, making sure we're all still together.

Tonights activity is story time with s'mores around the campfire. The rest of the week they have midday crafts planned, game night, a scavenger hunt, hayrides, and then a movie night Thursday night.

The movie night has always been my favorite. The camp staff members play a popular movie from a projector, kind of like at a drive in. Everyone brings their own chairs and blankets and the staff serve free popcorn.

The last night, Friday night, will be the actual day for the 100th year celebration. That's the main event that everyone is looking forward to, myself included.

Once we finally arrive to the front of the campground where the activity is taking place tonight, the recreation team already has the fire going. They placed multiple bales of hay in the shape of a circle around the fire pit for the kids to sit on.

The warm glow of the fire flickers in the background as I watch the kids scatter, already making new friends and getting settled on the hay bales.

"Do you remember when we used to do this, Gemma?"

"Of course I do," she replies with a grin. "My favorite time was when they did the Halloween campfire stories during the fall season. I had nightmares about the *boogeyman* for months."

I can't help but laugh, the sound genuine and free. "Okay, but same. Those were always the best."

The memories flood back—the way the campfire stories seemed to come alive with every twist and turn, the way we used to huddle close together as the wind rustled through the trees. I still remember how we would race back to our camper after the stories, hearts pounding from excitement... and maybe a little bit of fear.

I glance at Gemma, who's still smiling, probably lost in her own memories. "Do you ever wish we could go back to being those kids?" I ask her softly, even though I know the answer.

She looks over at me, her eyes glinting with that familiar mischievous spark. "What, you mean to the time when we didn't have to worry about laundry, bills, or bad hair days?" she teases, nudging me with her elbow.

I laugh again, the sound easy and natural between us. "Exactly."

I start grazing through the crowd to see if I recognize anyone and then my eyes meet a familiar pair of blue ones. Jesse Cooper. My heart skips a beat, and suddenly, the noise of the campfire and kids playing seems distant. It's just him.

A familiar smile spreads across his face, and before I know it, he's waving us over.

"I'll stay over here with Goose, you go ahead," Gemma instructs.

"Are you sure?"

"Positive." Gemma walks over to a bench and sits down with Goose.

I speed walk over to Jesse and he gives me a hug. "Hi stranger. I missed you."

"You miss me already? We were together yesterday, there's no way you aren't tired of me yet."

He pulls his face back to look at me, his expression soft and sincere. "Cora, I could never get tired of you."

Just as I open my mouth to reply, Charlie's voice cuts through the moment. "Break it up, lovebirds," he teases with a grin. "Don't you know there are little eyes and little ears around here?"

I laugh and pull back slightly, feeling the heat in my cheeks. I reach for Jesse's hand, giving it a light squeeze. "Very funny, Charlie," I say with a playful roll of my eyes. "It's good to see you too."

Charlie smirks, then looks around the campfire. "Where'd your sister run off to?" His brow furrows slightly as he scans the crowd. "I could've sworn I just saw her with Goose."

I glance over to where Gemma's sitting, then point toward the bench where she and Goose are. "They're over there."

She makes eye contact with me when she sees me pointing in her direction. Her eyes go wide and she immediately looks away and gets out her phone.

"Hmm," Charlie mutters, glancing over at the kids. "Well, I think Jenny and Harrison are friends now. They played together really well today."

I follow his gaze, and my heart warms as I watch Jenny sitting between my two boys, laughing at something one of them said.

"I'm glad they're finally warming up," I admit, my voice softening. "They had such a hard time with everything that happened with Nash. I was so worried they weren't going to make many friends when we moved."

"Well, it looks like you don't have to worry anymore." Jesse's voice is reassuring as he leans in and kisses my forehead. The simple gesture sends a wave of calm through me.

32
Coraline

EVERYTHING IS READY TO go, and it's time to make our way to the kick-off party. We've had a wonderful week of camping so far.

Jesse's visited the campsite every evening and has played with both of the kids. I had to leave to go to work every day for a couple of hours, but the kids have had a wonderful time with Granna and Pappy.

The Camp Willowbrooke 100th year celebration is being held at the entrance to the golf course. We all opt to ride our bikes down together instead of driving because we're so close to the location. It would almost be silly to drive down and have to fight for a place to park. Even Granna and Pappy are riding their bikes this time.

As soon as the party comes into view, my jaw drops. Jesse and his crew have gone above and beyond. This looks like something straight out of a movie.

There are carnival-style lights twinkling everywhere, and the entire area is filled with excitement. A Ferris wheel spins lazily in the distance, a carousel plays its cheerful tune, a fun slide waits for brave adventurers, and off to the side, I spot a Gravitron. I can't help but giggle to myself when I see it. Jesse and I got stuck inside of one of those at the county fair when we were in middle school.

There are multiple vendor tents, food trucks, and inflatables for the kids. I notice that the Scottsdale Diner has its own tent full of desserts made by no one other than Pamela.

Most of the vendors here run their own small businesses. Events like this give them a chance to really promote their products and establish more customers. The small company that sells my favorite candle, *Spice of Life*, is set up here too. I'll have to come back later and buy a few to stock up.

As we park our bikes in the bike rack, the smell of a kettle corn stand makes my mouth water. There's not many things that are better than good ol' kettle corn. I make a mental note to hit it up later too.

They have a main stage set up for music with a crowd already forming. Pappy starts making his way down through the crowd to get to the stage. He's supposed to open the ceremony in prayer before the first band performs.

"Mom, can we go ride some rides?" Harrison asks, his eyes wide with excitement.

"Please, Mama?" Michael adds, his face contorting into his best puppy-dog look.

I smile at them but shake my head. "Not yet, boys," I say gently. "I want to listen to Pappy open the ceremony, and then we can go play."

Granna steps up behind me, placing a hand on my shoulder. "I can take them, Coraline."

I glance back at her, a little relieved. "Are you sure you don't mind?" I ask.

Granna smiles warmly, her eyes twinkling. "Not at all. You enjoy the ceremony. I'll make sure they don't get into too much trouble."

"Thank you, Granna." I sigh in relief. "Boys, you all have to stay together. I'll come and find you after the band plays their first song."

"Thanks Mom!" They each take one of Granna's hands and off they go.

She waves me off with a wink, taking both boys' hands and leading them towards the rides. I watch them go, feeling a sense of calm wash over me as I turn back to the front of the celebration, ready for Pappy's speech to begin.

There are three bands total for tonight. The first band that's supposed to go on is a local church band. They're an old time bluegrass band that sings gospel music, but we love them anyway.

I look towards the crowd and my eyes crash with Jesse's. He's got his curly, dark hair styled and is rocking a five o'clock shadow. He's wearing a Camp Willowbrooke t-shirt with matching basketball shorts.

Charlie and John are standing beside of Jesse with their arms folded over their chests, both sporting smirks. Jesse rolls his eyes at them.

I'm a little surprised to see John here. Shae still hasn't told me anything yet. I've been trying to support her privacy as much as I can but I know that something has happened.

"Hello boys," I say with a wave, my voice light and playful.

"Hi Coraline," they respond in unison, a smile tugging at the corners of their mouths. "Hi Gemma."

"Hey, boys," Gemma replies and quickly looks away. Her cheeks tinged with a hint of pink. It's subtle, but I catch it.

"Excuse me, everyone. If I could please have your attention. We are going to be opening this celebration with prayer." The announcer steps back, and Pappy walks onto the stage.

We all bow our heads, and I listen intently to his opening prayer. His words are familiar, comforting, and grounding, but it's the quiet stillness that surrounds me that brings me the most peace.

As Pappy prays, I feel my heart swell with joy, and a sense of serenity I've been missing for so long fills me completely.

Tears prick at my eyes. I don't try to hold them back. Instead, I embrace them as a sign of gratitude—a reminder of how blessed I am to be standing here, to feel God's presence so strongly. He can show up anywhere and anytime and I'm so for thankful that.

Just as I let myself lean into the peace of the prayer, I feel Jesse's hand brush against mine. His touch is gentle and reassuring, a quiet anchor amidst the emotions swirling inside me. His hand closes around mine, giving me a tender squeeze.

I am so blessed to have a second chance, with my first love.

33
Coraline

THE SIX OF US listen to the first band play their opening song, which just so happens to be one of Pappy's favorites. Some of the music shows I went to in the city always started out slow and kind of awkward, but not here in Scottsdale. This band started out with a bluegrass bang and the crowd was really feeling the music.

I spot Mira and Henry Jacobs near the front of the crowd. They're hand in hand dancing to the music. Henry is twirling Mira around like she weighs nothing. The crowd starts to watch them and cheer them on. They're both laughing and having the time of their life.

Jesse catches me staring at them and the next thing I know, his hand was in mine and he's pulling me toward them and the "dance floor".

I didn't have any time to protest before he was twirling me around to the fast pace of the song. The steady rhythm of the bass, the twang of the banjo and the frantic sound of the fiddle guides our bodies as we keep up the pace to the song.

When the chorus plays, we switch partners and I linked arms with Henry. We spin around in a circle and the sound of our laughter spills over the loud music. After a few beats, we switch back to our original partners.

Other couples from the crowd start to gather all around us to join in on the fun too. I forgot how good it feels to just let go and dance. My face is starting to hurt from smiling so hard.

The summer air is thick with the smell of our sweat and the scent of the earth as we continue our dance. The crowd is getting larger and they're just as caught up in the melody of the song as we are.

As the last few chords of the song play out and the fiddle hits its last note, the crowd rides out their final wave of energy and erupts into a standing ovation. Jesse pulls me in for a hug as I attempt to catch my breath. My heart is pounding hard in my chest and I can feel sweat dripping down my back.

He presses a kiss to my cheek and I feel a tiny pang of guilt. It's been a long time since I've ever done anything like this without my kids. I know it's not wrong and that they're more than likely having a great time riding rides with Granna, but I still feel guilty. I can't explain it. Mom guilt is always something that I've experienced.

"This was fun and all guys but I've got to go find the boys," I say with a small smile. "I told them I would come find them after the first song. If you see Gemma, will you guys let her know where I went?"

"Absolutely," Charlie replies.

I turn to walk away and I feel Jesse's fingers brush against mine as we navigate out of the crowd together. I guess he's tagging along too. I look up at him and bravely take his hand in mine in front of everyone. The banjo starts up and the second song starts to play.

We continue to hold hands and make small talk while we look around for the kids and Granna. It feels like we're teenagers again. We used to go to the county fair together every fall and walk around just like this and talk about anything and everything. That seems like it was a lifetime ago now.

"Jess, how's your dad holding up?" As far as I know, Lloyd still hasn't heard much of anything from Keri and she skipped town.

"He's hanging in there," he shrugs. "All he can seem to talk about is the fishing trip we went on together. He really enjoyed spending time with us and the boys. It helped take his mind off of things at home."

I always liked Lloyd and I hate to see him hurting. I still don't understand how he got caught up with a woman like Keri. She has always hated my guts.

One of my biggest regrets in life is listening to her when she told me that I was holding Jesse back from living his life. We would still have been together when I found out I was pregnant with Harrison and our lives would be completely different.

We continue on our walk and I'm fairly certain the entire town of Scottsdale is in attendance this evening because it's so crowded. I still have yet to find the kids or Granna in this crowd.

I'll call her and check on them soon. I'm sure they're just busy riding rides or playing games and we just overlooked them.

We walk right in front of the food trucks and the aroma of the funnel cakes and deep fried food makes my mouth water. My stomach growls loudly.

"Hey Cora, do you want anything from the food truck? I'm starting to get a little hungry and I figured the kids will want something to snack on as well."

"Actually that sounds perfect. Can you get them some cotton candy and a lemonade for all of us?"

Jesse and I used to get a lemonade with as much sugar as possible and a funnel cake to share when we would go to the fair all those years ago.

"Sure thing." He presses a soft kiss to my lips and then joins the food truck line. It feels so natural to be with Jesse again, like this is how it's supposed to be.

While he was getting us our food and drinks, I decided to sit at one of the empty picnic tables and take out my phone to call Granna. The sun is starting to go down now and I'm starting to get a little worried.

No answer. My stomach drops and I know in my gut that something is wrong. Jesse starts to walk toward me with all of our goodies, but my appetite has completely disappeared.

"Jess, I don't know why, but I know something is wrong. Granna will not answer her phone, it's getting dark out and we still haven't seen them. Call it mothers intuition, but I cannot shake this feeling," I say while trying to catch my breath. I feel like I'm on the verge of a panic attack.

"Okay, slow down. I'm sure everything is fine. I'll alert my team and have them keep an eye out for them," he says as he tries to reassure me.

Jesse pulls out his walkie and makes an announcement. "Attention staff, this is Jesse. Does anyone copy? Over."

There was static and then a beep. "Charlie, loud and clear. Over."

"Emergency Medical Response Team, loud and clear. Over."

"Security, loud and clear. Over."

Jesse brings the walkie back to his mouth again and presses the button. "We haven't been able to find Cora's grandmother or our sons. Has anyone seen them recently? Over."

"Affirmative. I just recently saw them at the bathhouse. Over," the security team replied.

We aren't too far from there but I know that we walked by it at least two times and did not see them. I immediately turn towards the bathhouse and take off running.

My heart is beating so hard in my chest that it feels like it's going to break free. Time feels like it has slowed down. The worst case scenarios run through my mind as I run through the crowd. Did someone take them? Are they hurt?

After what feels like years, I finally reach the bathhouse. Granna is sitting on a bench by herself looking down at her feet.

"Granna, where are the boys? I tried to call you but you didn't answer."

No response.

"Granna? Are you okay?" I snap my fingers in front of her face.

Still no response.

I put my hand to her forehead and note that she's cool and clammy.

"Granna, can you hear me?" I note that she is also pale in color and her eyes are glassy.

Jesse runs up behind me and takes in the situation.

"Jess, I need you to walkie the emergency medical response team. I think Granna is having a low blood sugar episode. She's diabetic and I found her here alone. The boys are nowhere in sight."

I feel like I'm physically dissociating from my body as he makes the announcement on his walkie. I try my best to hold my composure. Granna has been a diabetic for as long as I can remember but has never had an episode like this. Not that I can recall anyways.

As soon as I spot the medical team approaching and I know that Granna will be in safe hands, I turn around and frantically start to search for my kids again.

I feel like the entire world is spinning at a thousand miles per hour and I can't focus. My only thoughts are about finding them. I know that I'm a trained medical professional, I recognize that I need to calm down and try to be rational, but I literally can't.

I attempt to search the crowd for my little boys but all I see is a sea full of people. The lights and sounds of the rides that initially made me excited, now make me feel overstimulated. I feel like I'm trapped in my own personal horror movie.

My eyes continue to dart from ride to ride and from person to person. Every second that passes feels like an *hour* too long.

There's no way that the boys would have left. They know better than to disappear.

My heart continues to sink as I realize that someone has to have taken them. I start to sob and at this point my fear is uncontrollable. I don't know what else to do.

I fall to my knees and start praying as hard and as fast as I can. I don't care who sees me. I don't care what anyone thinks.

I believe in a God that can do anything and I know he will bring my babies to me. I know that my God will hear me.

34
Jesse

How could such a perfect night turn into such a nightmare?

The emergency medical response team was able to check Granna's blood glucose level, which ended up being forty, and they treated her.

Apparently, she started a new medication and forgot to eat before she came to the event tonight. I know that it's not her fault, and I do not blame her for what happened, but now both of our boys are gone. It's like they vanished into thin air without a trace.

I pull out my walkie to make an announcement to all event workers and the security team. "Attention staff, this is Jesse Cooper. We have a Code Adam. This is not a drill. I repeat we have a Code Adam."

"There are two children missing. Harrison Jenkins, age six, and Michael Jenkins, age four. They were both last seen at the main bathhouse." I have to pause for a second as my voice breaks. I take a deep breath and exhale. "Everyone keep your eyes peeled. Nobody leaves this event and nobody gets in until we find these two boys. Over."

"Copy that. Over," a reply filters through the walkie.

The golf course is surrounded by the woods and the lake. The lake here is one of the biggest ones in the area and I don't even know if either of the boys can swim.

People get lost hiking multiple times a year, not only because the woods are so thick and lush, but because of the wildlife that's out there. I've seen a coyote on the campground before and we're in the region for bears and venomous snakes. Snakes are horrible this summer too. I shake my head to try to get rid of all the intrusive and negative thoughts.

I turn around to see Granna with her head in her hands crying. "I'm so sorry, Jesse. I don't think Cora will ever forgive me."

"It's not your fault. There's no way you could know that this was going to happen to you. We will find them." I pat her back. "I'm just glad you are okay now."

I turn and walk away from Granna. I start going up to members of the crowd and asking as many people as I can about the boys. I ask if anyone has seen them or has seen anything out of the ordinary. So far I'm not having any luck at all.

I spot Charlie, John, and Pappy running through the crowd to get to me.

"Have you found anything yet?" John asks.

"No. They could be anywhere with anyone. They may already be off of the property by now." A million horrific scenes flood my mind again as I think of what the boys could be going through. My hands start to tremble as adrenaline continues to flood through my body.

"Gemma is with Coraline. She's trying to help her calm down," Charlie adds. I cover my face with my hands and try to remember how to breathe.

"We will find them Jesse." John says as he puts his firm hand on my shoulder.

"Charlie and John, why don't you two go to the stage and announce the situation. I'll stay with Jesse and help him continue to search," Pappy suggests.

"That sounds like a good idea." I agree and put my hands on my hips. "I've got all emergency teams and staff members stopping people from leaving the event and they are monitoring the parking areas."

"We're on it." Charlie and John turn and start running in the direction of the stage.

Pappy turns to me after they're gone. "Son, do you mind if we pray together?"

"I think I'd very much like that."

We put our arms around each other and cry out in a desperate prayer. I start to feel God's presence all over me like I did earlier when I was with Cora. It was like a wave of calmness washed over me. All at once, I knew that everything was going to be okay.

"Jesse Cooper, do you copy? Over," a voice filters through the speaker in my pocket.

I pull out of Pappy's embrace and pull out my walkie. "Jesse Cooper, loud and clear. Over."

"We found them."

35
Coraline

I'M SITTING ON A bench with Gemma as she attempts to help me calm down. Rationally, I know what I need to do. But it's so much harder when you're actually going through the situation and it's your own kids who are missing.

My hands are shaking in my lap while I hold on to my prayer quilt. I always keep it on me now, no matter where I am.

I can't think of anyone who would want to take them other than a pure monster. I mutter the same prayer over and over again. I give my all to God amidst the chaos.

I look up from my prayer quilt and see Pappy and Jesse running over to get to us.

"Cora, they found them," Jesse says in a rush. "Let's go get our babies."

I jump up out of my seat and take off after him. I don't know where we're going but I know that I can't stop until I see their faces with my own eyes.

Sirens wail in the distance, but all I can hear is the pounding of my heart. It's racing so fast I swear it might burst. Flashing red and blue lights spin across the scene, casting frantic shadows. Police cars are everywhere. My mind is drowning in the endless spiral of what-ifs—what if they're hurt? What if I'm too late?

Then I hear it—

"MAMA!"

One word. One voice. My world snaps back into focus.

I spin toward the sound, legs moving before I can even think. I run across the pavement, dodging between paramedics and officers until I see them.

My babies.

I fall to my knees and gather them into my arms, clutching them like I'll never let go. Jesse reaches us seconds later, wrapping his arms around all three of us. We're a knot of tears, arms, breathless sobs—and love.

Thank you, God.

I press my face into their hair, breathing them in, as tears slip silently down my cheeks. Relief floods every part of me, washing away the fear. They're here. In my arms. Alive. Safe.

"What happened?" I finally manage to ask.

I'm not ready to break the hug yet, I'm afraid that if I let go of them that they're going to disappear again.

"Michael had to pee and Granna was acting really strange so I told him to go ahead and go to the bathroom," Harrison said. "He had been gone for a long time and Granna was still acting funny, so I went inside to check on him."

"When I was looking for him in the stalls, I saw Nash. The bad man."

My stomach drops like a stone.

"Are you sure it was him?" My voice comes out quieter than I mean it to.

What is he doing out of jail? How did he get out? Why was he here?

"It was! Daddy told me that he wanted it to be just like the old times," Michael says, his little voice trembling now. "He said that I needed to go with him, but I told him about my new daddy. That made him very angry."

"Oh sweetheart," I cry and hold him tighter against my chest.

"The bad man was trying to take my bubby and was dragging him out the back door. So, I went up to him and tried to get my brother back," Harrison continued. "I was swinging as hard and as fast as I could at him and then some lady grabbed me. They made us leave with them and get inside of an old, stinky car."

"They put us in the back seat and told us to lay on the floor and be real quiet. Daddy said that if we were good he would take us to get superhero ice cream. I knew that was wrong because I remembered you said he was not a good person and bad people don't take good people to get superhero ice cream," Michael said while he pointed his finger up.

"I also remembered what my teacher at church told me to do anytime I felt scared," Harrison said, his voice soft but steady. "So I laid down in the back seat, hugged my bubby, and prayed."

He glanced up at me, eyes wide. "When I started to pray, the strange lady in the front seat got really mad."

"When I finished praying," he continued, "a policeman knocked on the window. He asked the bad man and the strange lady if they had seen two little boys."

He paused, letting the moment hang. "And something told me in my mind to scream. So I did—as loud as I could."

"The policeman heard me. He saw us. Then he took the bad man and the strange lady away." He's smiling now, proud of himself.

"I'm so very proud of you boys," I whisper. "You both are so brave. I love you so much."

After I finally felt level headed, I went to speak to the police officer who found them. He confirmed that the entire story that Harrison and Michael told to me was true.

It turns out that Nash was bailed out of jail a few days ago by the "strange lady" who turned out to be Jesse's mother, Keri. Why on God's green earth she decided to bail him out of jail and hook up with him is a complete mystery to me.

It's an even bigger mystery as to why she wanted to help kidnap my son. It literally made zero sense to me other than the fact that she wanted to hurt me like she was hurting.

Apparently when Jesse approached her about hiding Harrison from him, she left town and then proceeded to look up what jail Nash was in and paid him a visit one day. They bonded over their hatred for me over the weeks she was gone. That's why Lloyd hadn't heard anything from her and why Nash had stopped harassing me.

Finding out that your wife has been hiding a grandchild from you is bad enough but then to add on an affair and attempted kidnapping? How do you move on from that?

Keri and Nash have both been arrested tonight and the officer says that they will be charged with aggravated kidnapping of a child under the age of fourteen on two counts.

36
Jesse

IT'S OCTOBER, MY FAVORITE month of the year. I've always loved the season of fall and all of the things that come with it, especially football season.

This will be my first time celebrating Halloween and going trick-or-treating with Harrison and Michael.

Camp Willowbrooke usually has a big Halloween festival for the town and campers. The people who are camping during the festival decorate their campers and campsites.

It's highly competitive and some of our campers go all out and create little scary booths and tents for people to walk through.

Last year, Henry and Mira Jacobs brought supplies with them. They built and disassembled an entire pirate ship and deck just for the week of the festival.

During the trick-or-treat time, they both dressed up like pirate zombies and were "in character" until it was over. They were last year's winners and won an entire year's worth of free camping.

With everything that happened with my mom and Nash, I've actually been debating on not having the event this year. The only reason I decided to continue on with it was because the kids are so excited about it.

We're not going to be actively camping on site because my house is so close. We will however, still take a bike ride everyday throughout the campground to watch the campsites transform.

"Boys, do you want to help me set the table and get the drinks ready before your mom gets here?" I ask as I place a *Spice of Life* candle in the middle of the dinner table.

I pick up my handy dandy torch lighter, because what other kind of lighter would a man keep in his house, and light the candle.

Every time I smell the sweet, fall aroma it takes me back to being sixteen and madly in love with Cora. The only thing that's different now is our age.

"Sure thing, Dad!" Harrison yells from the kitchen.

Cora had me keep both kids today, at my house, while she worked at the clinic. What she doesn't know is that we have a surprise waiting for her. Both of the kids helped me plan everything. I even let them pick out the dinner entree and dessert.

Harrison has on a blue chef's hat and apron. Michael has on a matching set—but in the color green.

They both requested that we make their favorite food—dinosaur chicken nuggets with barbecue sauce, french fries, and brownies with icing. The meal of champions.

We made the brownies earlier around lunch time so we would have time to ice them before Cora made it here.

She should be getting here any minute and I'm starting to get a little anxious. She thinks that she's picking up the kids and going back home—at this point I think she knows me better than that.

Ever since she came back into town we've had a hard time staying apart and an even harder time saying goodbye.

I grab a large bowl from the cabinet and fill it up with ice from my ice machine. I only like to keep the "good ice" in my kitchen. Cora keeps telling me that I might be anemic because of how much I love to eat the ice, I disagree.

I hand the bowl to Harrison and we walk into the dining room.

Michael takes his blue dinosaur cup and scoops out the ice. He attempts to put the ice in our cups and ends up dumping most of it on the table and in the floor.

"I'm so glad you don't get mad at me like my other daddy used to," Micheal says as he looks up at me and smiles.

I bend down so that my face is level with his. "Bud, I want you to know that I will never do anything to hurt you, your brother, or your mama. I love all three of you and I never want you to be afraid of me."

"I love you too," he replies and gives me a high five.

Since the three of them came into my life, everything has changed for the better. I can't imagine living another day that didn't involve Cora and our boys. I don't ever want to go back to how things were before they moved back to Scottsdale.

Tonight is going to be perfect. I've been praying about the best time to propose to Cora. She gave her heart to the Lord and then he gave her back to me. I couldn't be more blessed.

I want to wake up every day beside her beautiful face. I want to experience all that life has to offer me from here on out with her and the kids by my side. We've waited this long to come back together, so what are we waiting on now?

The oven alarm interrupts my thoughts and I get up to check the food.

I'm halfway to the kitchen when I hear the front door open.

"Boys?" Cora says in a sing-song voice.

"In here, Mom," they both say at the same time.

I hear her light footsteps as she walks into the dining room. I turn around so I can go greet her.

Before she can see me, I tap my pocket to make sure the ring is still in place. This has been one of the hardest secrets to keep.

I spot her embracing both kids, one in each arm. Her strawberry blonde hair is pulled up into a loose ponytail and she's wearing the pink pair of scrubs that she knows are my favorite pair on her.

Her honey colored eyes collide with mine she blushes. I love it when she does that.

"Hey sweetheart," I say while giving her a knowing look. "Did you have a good day at work?"

"Yeah, it wasn't bad," she says as she smiles up at me. "What are you all up to? Something smells... interesting."

"We made you dinner!" Michael says enthusiastically.

"Awe, that's so sweet," she says as she kisses Michael and Harrison each on the cheek. She walks over to me and gives me a soft kiss on the lips. Both boys make pretend gagging noises.

Suddenly, the smoke detector starts to alarm.

As soon as I hear it, I remember that I never pulled the chicken nuggets out of the oven.

Lucy runs inside of the house from her doggy door and starts howling like a wolf from the kitchen.

I run into the room after her, while smoke fills the area. I scramble around to get the oven mitts on my hands.

I frantically pull the baking sheet out of the oven and throw it into the sink.

The food was not actively on fire, but it was smoking pretty heavily and is completely charred. I scrunch up my face in disgust as the foul odor penetrates my nose and my mood.

So much for a perfect dinner.

Cora runs into the kitchen behind me and starts opening up windows. She grabs a towel and fans the smoke away from the detector and towards the windows to try to help the room air out.

I turn and look at Cora and she's got her hands over her mouth. She's hysterically laughing.

I can't help but join in on the laughter. We were brought back into each other's life over a broken oven from burnt cookies and...here we are again. Only this time there's nothing wrong with the oven, just poor time management.

The smoke detector finally stops alarming and we try to catch our breath from laughing. She has actual tears in her eyes.

I walk over to her to wipe them away. I feel God's presence in that moment urging me to do what I had been praying about.

"Well, I've been putting this off for the perfect moment but I'm quickly realizing that there never will be a perfect time. I can't wait any longer." I get down on one knee and take her hands in mine.

"Coraline Jennings, I had a much more romantic gesture planned that didn't include burnt chicken nuggets and smoke alarms, but there's something I want to say. I have loved you ever since I was a teenager. When I fell for you, I fell hard and with my entire heart. When you left me, I didn't know how to move on with my life."

I wipe a tear out of my eye.

"I never stopped loving you. I want to love you until I take my last breath, if you'll allow me to."

I turn to the boys and give them the signal. Harrison and Michael come and kneel on both sides of me. I pull the little black velvet box out of my pocket.

I take a deep, shaky breath and open the box.

"Coraline Jennings, will you marry me?"

"Pretty please, with a cherry on top?" Michael adds.

I can see the big, fat tears forming in Cora's eyes. She nods her head up and down.

"Yes!" Harrison yells. "My mom and dad are getting married!"

37
Coraline

"Come on boys, make sure to grab your bags!" I shout from the porch.

I look down at my left hand and the diamond that sits on my ring finger. I still feel like I'm dreaming and that someone is going to pinch me and wake me up. God has continued to bless me and my family and it just doesn't feel real.

Harrison zooms past me and stands by the steps on the porch.

"How does my wig look mom?" He says as he strikes his best pirate pose.

Harrison is wearing a long, curly, black wig with a maroon pirate hat on top. He has matching pirate style pants on with long white socks and black shoes. He's even wearing a fake mustache, which shocked me, and has a fake pirate hook on his hand.

"I love it! You look perfect! How's my dress?" I twirl around in a circle and then curtsy.

I'm wearing a light blue dress with a matching bow tied around my middle. I have my hair curled and pulled halfway up with another bow.

"Shiver me timbers! You look good, ya scallywag!" Harrison has been practicing his pirate voice all month.

"What's going on out here?" Michael gasps dramatically.

He comes out on the porch and lands in a 'spider-man' pose.

He's wearing a green t-shirt that's long enough to be a short dress with matching green leggings. He reaches up to straighten his angular green cap and pats it to make sure that the red feather is still in place. Then he pulls out his small, toy dagger.

"Mom! Get away from him before he guts you like a fish!" We all three break out into laughter and the boys pretend to fight with their pirate hook and dagger.

The weather this time of year is hit or miss, but today it's sixty degrees out and very pleasant. I know that as soon as the sun goes down it will drop down into the forties so I made sure to pack extra jackets and a blanket in my backpack.

After I break up the fake fight, the three of us climb on our bikes and ride over to Jesse's lakeside "mansion". It's not really a mansion, but I joke with him and call it one because it's too big for one man and a dog.

We just got engaged the other day and like any excited couple to-be-wed, we've been discussing wedding ideas and where we're going to live. It only made sense for us to move into his house after the wedding.

If I could pick the perfect house for my family, it would be his. I know Jesse helped to design and build it a few years ago and it's just so cool to me how God knew that it would be ours one day. I firmly believe that God had us in mind when he helped Jesse design it.

Jesse's sitting on the porch in his costume with Lucy at his feet. He has on a blue and white striped t-shirt, a red toboggan, matching blue pants and tan sandals.

Lucy's wearing a white lace bonnet—I'm so proud of her for keeping it on.

We're going trick-or-treating at Camp Willowbrooke as a family. The kids wanted to wear matching costumes, which is something we've never been able to do before.

We picked out our costumes from one of our favorite movies, 'Peter Pan'. The kids' trick-or-treat bags have a quote from the movie on it with an outline of all the characters flying in the sky.

Granna and Pappy are camping out on the campground with Gemma, so we will for sure stop by and visit with them after trick-or-treating. They wouldn't tell us their theme and have been keeping their decorations covered with sheets so we couldn't spy on them on our evening bike rides.

I was tempted to stay with them overnight but Harrison is in school now and is still adjusting. I'm also still working on trusting Granna with my kids again. I know and understand that she in no way shape or form meant for my kids to be in harm's way, but I'm just not ready yet. I have forgiven her and we did talk things out but I just need more time.

"You guys look awesome! Especially you, *Wendy Darling*." Jesse says with a wink.

"Are you ready, Dad?" Michael asks.

"Yep! Let's roll." He grabs Lucy's leash and he mounts his bicycle to join us.

By the end of the summer Michael was able to ride a bike without training wheels, thanks to Jesse's help. I'm so proud of them.

I'm also thankful that God made room in Jesse's heart for a son that was not his own blood. He loves him just as fiercely as he does Harrison.

Jesse rides his bike in front of us with Lucy trotting along beside him. The boys follow next, side by side, and I ride at the tail end. I like to have eyes on all four of them at all times even though we're just going two minutes down the road.

The color of the leaves on the trees and the aroma of all the campfires from the campsite warms my heart. I can't help but to admire God's wonderful creation and the beauty of it.

The season of autumn reminds me that death can be cold and dreary, but it can also be warm and beautiful too. The leaves on the trees are pretty in color because they're dying and moving on to the next part of their story.

But, when spring comes around in a few months, we are blessed with new life and it will begin again. This is also true in my own journey with Christianity. I was so sinful that I felt like I was dead inside. Then, Jesus came into my life and everything feels new and promising.

We had an uneventful bike ride, no one got hurt and we were able to just enjoy each-others company and the scenery. I couldn't ask for anything more.

As we approached the entrance to Camp Willowbrooke, I developed butterflies in my stomach. I'm excited and nervous at the same time. I have to keep reminding myself that God is in control and Nash and Keri are in jail.

The entrance of the campground by the Camp Willowbrooke sign is decorated with fodder shocks, two life size scarecrows, and various shades of mums. There's also a big orange sign that has been recently staked in the ground that reads; "Enter if you dare and trick-or-treaters beware. Goblins and ghouls run amuck on All Hallows' eve. Good luck!"

We ride down the first familiar loop of the campground and start to scope out the costumes and campsites. We see a few other families with their kids out and unloading from their vehicles. The sun is just now starting to set and I know that this campground will be completely full when it's dark.

Granna and Pappy are at site seven so they're not too far away. The kids trick or treat at site number one which is where Pamela Collins and her family are staying.

Pamela has on a giant blonde, curly wig and a vibrant, pink jumpsuit that's covered in silver jewels and rhinestones. The jumpsuit is long sleeved and has a v cut front. When she raises her arms she has strings of rhine-stones hanging off of them. Pamela also has on silver cowboy boots and a matching hot pink cowboy hat. She honestly looks like she just stepped out from a Nashville bachelorette party and I love it. Pamela even has a speaker playing *"Jolene"* and her little dog has on a pink vest to match along with her.

"Good evenin' folks." Pamela says in her best country accent. "Happy Halloween!"

"Happy Halloween!" Jesse and I reply at the same time. "You look fantastic!" I add.

"Thank you doll baby," she winks at me. "Come here boys! I've got all kinds of candy and you're more than welcome to some. That is, if you know the magic words." She crosses her arms and raises an eyebrow.

I hope I'm as cool as she is when I'm in my seventies. I mean seriously where does this woman get her energy from?

"Trick-or-treat!" The boys say at the same time. Pamela gives them a handful of candy from her large, bedazzled candy bowl and then we are on our way.

We hit spot two, three, and four which are each decorated with typical Halloween inflatable blow ups and skeleton decor.

When we reached spot five my mouth drops open.

Henry and Mira Jacobs are dressed up like *Marty McFly* and *Doc Brown*! They transformed a car into looking almost identical to the one from the *'Back to the Future'* movies.

"Jesse! Do you see what I see?" I say while raising my eyebrows and smiling. He's totally going to freak out. Henry and Mira had also covered their decorations up all week so we didn't know what they were building.

"That. Is. The. Coolest. Thing. I've. Ever. Seen. In. My. Entire. Life." He came to a complete stop and was absolutely mesmerized. *'Back to the*

Future' is one of Jesse's comfort movies that he watches all the time. He was literally stuck in his tracks and couldn't stop gaping at their campsite.

"I've got to get a picture of this. Go stand by them!" I take out my phone to grab a few quick pictures. Jesse was acting like a little school girl, it was hilarious.

We finally made it to Granna and Pappy's campsite, and Michael squealed in pure delight.

They had transformed their entire site into a *Mario Kart* world.

Pappy stood proudly in a red t-shirt and blue jean overalls, a red cap perched on his head—he was Mario, through and through. Granna looked absolutely regal in a pink ball gown, a blonde wig cascading down her shoulders, and a crown resting perfectly on top. Princess Peach had entered the chat.

Gemma was rocking a Luigi costume—green t-shirt, blue overalls, and a comically large fake mustache that kept sliding down her face.

And Goose? Goose was a *green shell*. He somehow had a little turtle shell harnessed to his back, waddling around like he was waiting to be launched.

When Lucy spotted him, she calmly walked over, circled once, and plopped down beside him like it was the most normal thing in the world.

"*THIS IS AWESOME!*" Harrison yells at the top of his lungs.

Without another word, he takes off sprinting toward the campsite.

Granna and Pappy had gone *all out*. They spray-painted huge PVC pipes bright green to look like warp tunnels, and scattered fun little props from the game all around the site. The golf cart? Transformed into *Bowser's* racing car, complete with spikes and flames down the sides.

But the real showstopper?

A towering replica of *Princess Peach's* castle—at least two feet taller than me. The roof is painted pink with red flags fluttering from the turrets. It looks like it came straight out of the game.

"How did you guys do all of this? This is amazing!" I said, still in total awe.

When Jesse told me everyone went all out for Halloween, I didn't realize he meant *this* kind of all out. I can't imagine how the judges are supposed to pick just one winner—we're only at site seven, and there are at least thirty more to go.

Granna smiled and took my hand in hers, giving it a gentle squeeze.

"We have two little grandsons that mean the world to us. When you're motivated, you can do anything you set your mind to," she said, her eyes twinkling.

"And we had a little help from Gemma," she added, dropping her voice just enough to make it feel like a secret. "Charlie owed her a favor, so he pitched in and helped your grandfather."

My eyebrows shot up. *Interesting.*

Harrison and Michael were beaming, practically bouncing with excitement.

"Mom, this is the best Halloween *ever!*" Harrison shouted.

Epilogue

I PACE BACK AND forth in the master bedroom, trying to calm my racing nerves. Today is the day I become Mrs. Coraline Cooper. Nothing has ever felt so right.

Some might say we're rushing things—especially after everything that happened last summer with Nash and Keri—but I don't care. This is the moment I've dreamed of since I was a little girl.

This is the same boy I fell in love with when I was fourteen—my first love, my first kiss. And somehow, I love him even more than I did back then. I never knew that was possible.

A few weeks ago, Nash was officially sentenced to life in prison, with no chance for parole. He'll never see the light of day again.

Keri, on the other hand, was sentenced to twenty years.

As for Lloyd—Jesse's dad—he was granted a divorce from her, and he's been nothing short of amazing. He's become the best papaw my kids could ask for, and I can't help but feel a little grateful for that.

I take a deep breath and check my reflection for what feels like the thousandth time today. My dress has a deep V-neckline, that hugs my chest and waist before flowing outward, like something straight out of a fairytale—a real-life ballgown.

The sheer tulle shimmers softly, decorated with white lace flowers that are scattered throughout the entire gown. I was going for timeless, yet modern look, with just a touch of fairytale magic.

And right now? I feel just like a real-life *Disney* princess.

My strawberry blonde hair is curled half up and half down in loose, voluminous waves. The top half of my hair is twisted and braided back to give an elegant touch.

I opted not to wear a traditional veil over my face, but I still wanted one pinned in my hair that flows down my back.

My sister, Gemma, did my bridal makeup. She blended various shades of brown and a touch of shimmery gold on my eyelids to make them pop. The winged eyeliner gave it a bold, dramatic effect, and she finished the look with false eyelashes that made my eyes stand out even more. For my lips, we kept it simple with a soft, natural pink.

I look down at my flower bouquet and squeeze the piece of fabric that's wrapped around the stems. I say a silent prayer to help ease my nerves.

I had my prayer quilt incorporated into my bouquet. It's been with me through every major, life changing event since Pappy gave it to me all those years ago.

I may not have realized it back then, but it has been such a blessing and piece of comfort for me to know that I always have a savior that I can count on no matter the place, time or situation. God is always there.

The venue that we picked is right in Jesse's yard, nestled perfectly between the rental house and his house, which is now ours. The past month has been a whirlwind of moving everything from the rental house into our new home.

Harrison and Michael no longer have to share a room now that we're all living together. They've loved every minute of it—picking out decorations for their new rooms, painting walls, and making the space their own.

The kids will also have their own game room in Jesse's man cave/garage. Over the past year, they've spent so much time there with him, especially during football and basketball season. Jesse's been teaching them about sports, and they've been soaking up every minute of his attention.

"It's time, sis," Gemma says, taking my hands in hers.

I close my eyes and take a deep breath. The nerves have melted away. I don't feel anxious anymore. I know, without a shadow of a doubt, that the man standing at the end of the aisle loves me with his whole heart, and that he was handpicked for me and our two sons.

"Let's do this." I say, nodding once.

I glance out the window one last time. The sun has just begun to set behind the trees, casting a soft golden glow across everything. Flowers and twinkling lights are strung everywhere, creating a magical atmosphere. A small crowd of our closest friends and family is making their way to their seats.

It looks like something straight out of a romcom. I almost feel like Bella from *Twilight*—standing here, about to marry my one true love. Except, this is real life, and Jesse is definitely the farthest thing from a sparkly vampire.

The wedding party is lined up and ready to go. I stay hidden in the doorway of the bedroom until the last of the party descends down the steps and out onto the front porch.

Up until this point, the only people who have actually seen me are just my bridesmaids and my flower girl. I haven't seen Jesse today, we aren't superstitious, but we didn't want to jinx anything. Just in case.

The music begins to play out of the speakers, signaling the start of the ceremony. I get goosebumps all over my arms when I hear it. My eyes are already welling up with unshed tears.

We chose an instrumental version of the first song we ever slow-danced to—*A Thousand Years.*

I can't help but get emotional from thinking about how far we've come since then and how much our love has grown and changed.

Gemma, my maid of honor, is the first to walk down the aisle with Charlie by her side as Jesse's best man. Next are Shae and John, arm in arm.

I notice that John gives Shae a small kiss to her forehead before they step forward together. She leans into his touch, and I can't help but smile. They tied the knot this past spring.

Jenny, Charlie's daughter, walks down the aisle as our flower girl. She does a perfect job of taking her time distributing the white rose petals as with a big smile on her face. She stops every so often to make sure everyone is looking at her and is paying attention.

Next in line are Michael and Harrison, both serving as ring bearers. I wanted them to have something to do together, something special. Each of them carries a small briefcase, and their "Ring Security" badges are proudly displayed. Of course, they're both wearing black sunglasses, a decision Michael insisted on because he thought it made them look cooler. I caved, of course.

They walk side by side until they reach Jesse. Once they reach him, they dramatically take off their sunglasses and give the briefcases to him. After the rings are "secure" they turn and run like wild animals to their seats by Granna. At least they behaved while they walked down the aisle.

The music stops when they sit down and changes to an instrumental version of 'Can't Help Falling in Love'.

I take a few deep breaths in and out.

I know that it's now my turn to go now.

Being the center of attention has never been my thing, but this is the only wedding I plan on ever having and I want it to be special. There's no turning back.

When we initially rehearsed, I was supposed to take my time walking down the aisle. But today, as soon as my eyes find Jesse's piercing blue ones, I feel like I need to take off and run to him.

My legs betray me and I start speed walking.

He looks so handsome it almost hurts. His dark hair is perfectly curly and messily styled, just like always. He's wearing a dark grey suit, a crisp white button-down, and a bowtie. Both of his hands are clasped together, and his foot is tapping nervously.

I still can't believe that he's all mine and I get to spend forever with him.

At one point in my life, when I was at my lowest low, I believed that I didn't deserve a happy ending. And then God stepped in and rescued me and brought me here, to this very moment.

I haven't even looked around to see who is here or who isn't. Right now, all I care about is getting to Jesse.

When I make it halfway down the aisle, he starts crying and I realize that I am too. In fact, I can almost guarantee that there's not a dry eye in this place.

Once I finally reach him, I give my bouquet to Gemma and embrace her. She was the first friend I ever had. Sisters are special and I'm lucky that she's mine. I can only pray that my sons are as close as we are when they grow up.

I look over her shoulder and notice that Pappy is dabbing his eyes with his pocket handkerchief. I turn from Gemma and embrace Pappy next.

"I love you babygirl. You look so beautiful and I am so very proud of you." He kisses me on the cheek and then pulls away.

I take a step back and walk to Jesse. I grab both of his hands in mine and stare up at him.

Pappy begins his part of the ceremony.

I don't hear half of what he says. I'm too focused on Jesse and the fact that this is really happening. It feels like any minute I'm going to wake up and realize that this was all a dream.

We repeat the vows back to each other and now it's time for the big kiss to seal the deal. Jesse takes my face in both of his hands and presses his lips to mine in a soft, sensual kiss. Then, he moves both of his hands to my lower back as I wrap one arm around his neck.

He dips me backwards, just like we practiced, with our lips never parting. It's absolutely perfect. The crowd of our family and friends erupt out in cheers and I even hear a few whistles.

Once we break the kiss, we turn around and face the crowd, hand in hand. Our exit song starts to play and Jesse scoops me up into his arms and carries me all the way back down the aisle.

I'm so grateful that we ended up together after all.

Acknowledgements

I want to start off by thanking God for laying this story on my heart. Without his guidance, none of this would have been possible.

To my loving husband of seven years, thank you for listening to me talk about all things book related. Thank you for loving me the way you do and for always being supportive, even when I doubt myself.

To my sister, Madyson, thank you for always providing honest feedback. Anytime I sent you something about my story, you always provided some sort of redirection or feedback. I could not have done this without your help, love, and support! Also, congratulations on graduating college! I'm so very proud of you!

To my best friends, Megan and Emilie, thank you for listening to me rant and for providing feedback and ideas. You guys keep me sane amidst the chaos of my life. I love you both!

To my mom, thank you for always pushing me to achieve my goals in life and for always reading to me when I was a child. You and dad always supported my love for reading and I wouldn't be where I'm at today without that support. I love you.

To my mother-in-law, Kelli, and my sister-in-law, Britani (Aunt "B"), thank you for watching my children so that I had extra time to write and revise. You guys are the best! I love you guys!

To my Nanny in heaven, thank you for always taking me to church and making sure that I had a relationship with God. You were my prayer warrior and my inspiration. I miss you so much.

About the author

Alexis Vance is a full time mother, wife, and nurse with a dream of becoming an acclaimed author. She has been an avid reader for her entire life and is now making her dream a reality.

Her passion is to spread the love of God and help others grow closer to him through her stories.

When she's not reading or writing, she enjoys attending church with her family and camping with her kids.

If you want to follow along with her writing journey, you can find/contact her on any of the social media platforms below.

Instagram: @alexisvancewrites

TikTok: @alexisvancewrites

Goodreads: Together After All

Facebook Page: Alexis Vance Writes

Website: https://alexisvancewrites.my.canva.site/